HEART-BREAK ME

USA TODAY BESTSELLING AUTHOR
T.L. SMITH

Copyright T.L Smith 2020
Heartbreak Me by T.L Smith

All Rights Reserved

This book is a work of fiction. Any references to real events, real people, and real places are used fictitiously. Other names, characters, places, and incidents are products of the Author's imagination and any resemblance to persons, living or dead, actual events, organizations or places is entirely coincidental. All rights are reserved. This book is intended for the purchaser of this book ONLY. No part of this book may be reproduced or transmitted in any form or by any means, graphic, electronic, or mechanical, including photocopying, recording, taping, or by any information storage retrieval system, without the express written permission of the Author. All songs, song titles and lyrics contained in this book are the property of the respective songwriters and copyright holders.

WARNING

This book contains sexually explicit scenes and adult language and may be considered offensive to some readers. This e-book is intended for adults ONLY. Please store your files wisely, where they cannot be accessed by under-aged readers.
Cover – Outlined with love
Photographer- Michelle Lancaster photography
Edited – Swish Editing
Editor - Ink Machine Editing
Proofread – Lisa Edward

BLURB

He kidnapped me.

That was how I met Atlas Hyde.

A man known by many names and admired by all.

But most didn't know he was ruthless, conniving, and always got what he wanted.

No matter the cost.

I was a good girl.

Never in trouble with the law.

Never took drugs.

Always did precisely what was expected of me.

Even with his hand around my throat and words that cut sharper than knives, I couldn't help but wonder what happened to this beautiful man to make him that way.

That wonder disappeared when he threatened to kill my sister if I didn't follow his dark demands.

The good girl I once knew had now been buried alive beneath this game of hatred and lust.
And I had a feeling Atlas Hyde never lost.

CHAPTER ONE

Theadora

My breath shakes. How is that even possible? To have your breath shake? Shit!

Rough hands shove me, and I fall to my knees. My tied hands shoot out to catch me before I hit the ground. If it's rough, I'm afraid they may bleed.

Really, Theadora, that's what you're worried about?

I shake my thoughts away as I hear a laugh. I am unsure if I should sit up straight or stay bent over—I'm wearing a skirt that's way too short to stay this way—but if they wanted to do something to me, my guess is they would have by now. And so far, all they have done is tie me up, put a beanie on my head that covers my eyes, and throw me in a car.

"This is her!" A deep voice grumbles, which makes me sit up straight as it rumbles through my chest. I glance up to see this man, but then realize there's absolutely no reason at all to do so, considering I cannot see with the black beanie over my head effectively blocking my vision.

My hands are still tied in front of me, but they're no longer touching the ground, which is a hard surface. Cement maybe? I can't really tell.

"Yes, her." I'm kicked forward again, this time I'm not fast enough to stop the impact of my face meeting the floor. My forehead cracks as it makes contact, and my eyes squeeze shut as a burst of pain shoots through me.

"Gentle," that gruff voice states. "I don't want to break her…" I swallow as he pauses, "… yet."

Hands push me back, making me sit on my doubled back legs while one hand wraps around my throat and tightens.

This is the part where I should be screaming. I should be doing something, anything to fight this man. Except my body doesn't want to. Instead, it locks and freezes at his touch.

I've heard stories of this happening, how your

body locks up, even though you should be running, screaming, anything to get yourself free. I didn't believe it was possible until this very second. How can your fight or flight response *not* kick in?

I'm a good girl, having never done anything bad in my life.

"Boss, we can dispose of her easily enough."

Something snaps in me. "No." It's croaky, but I manage to squeak out the word.

The hands around my throat don't move, but his breath I can feel and smell through the beanie has a minty scent as he leans in closer to me.

"No," he says. "Do you even know why you are here, Theadora?" This man says my name as if he knows me. I don't know him—that voice, I would remember it. Trying to analyze him will do me no good. I can't see his reactions, so I go with gut instinct about what I want to say.

"No," I say because I have absolutely no idea why I am here. Which makes this situation even worse because I can be clumsy and forgetful. But for me to have done something to put me in this situation where they are talking of physically harming me? No. That's not something I've done.

"Maybe you should ask Lucy."

I pull back at his words, finally trying to free myself from his grasp. He holds me in place, the pressure hardening at my movement. "So, you know now, don't you?" I hear him take a deep breath, breathing me in.

"Where is she?" I ask with more venom than I thought I could muster. I feel the tears welling in my eyes, which I can't reach to wipe away, so they fall helplessly down my cheek and soak into my beanie.

"So, that got your attention." He pulls back. Well, I think he does, as I can no longer smell his breath near my face, and his hand on my throat loosens until it drops away completely. "Theadora! You don't mind if I call you that now, do you?"

I try to keep my smart-ass mouth shut at his words.

"Look, you're learning, much faster than Lucy did."

A small, shaky cry leaves me as heavy footsteps surround me. Hands reach under my arms and pull me up roughly, so I am standing on my own two feet.

"Where is she?" I ask the one who is doing all the talking. I can't tell where he is now that his hands aren't touching my throat, but my guess is he's in charge, so I direct my voice to where I assume he's standing

"Lucy stole over a million dollars from me,

Theadora. You *will* help me get that back. Or else Lucy will forget to breathe."

My mouth opens wide in shock at his words.

A million dollars? Fuck.

How?

Why?

So many questions.

And the last but most important one.

How the fuck am I meant to get that much money?

I'm smart. I earn good money managing one of the busiest clothing companies in the world, but I don't come near to earning that. And my savings is next to nothing, since I just bought my first home.

"Do you understand me, Theadora?"

My brain is too busy trying to figure out how to pull together that much money. Selling my house won't even give me half, and Lucy has no assets or money. Our parents died a long time ago, so it's just Lucy and me.

"How long do I have?" I ask.

The beanie is ripped from my face, my blonde hair, which was being held back, now sticks to my lips and I push it away with my tongue. My eyes are blurry, and I can hardly make anything out as he starts talking again, so I close my eyes and listen to his voice.

"You have one month, Theadora."

My heart drops, and I open my eyes, zoning in on that voice.

The man standing in front of me is not what I expected. Actually, he is anything but. If I saw him walking down the street I would stop to stare. If he were one of my company models, I would have stayed the whole shoot instead of instructing what I want, then leaving like I normally would.

No. This man? He is an attractive bad man, nothing more.

But despite his eyes that seem to stare straight through me, his hair is best described as scorched chestnut in color and appears tangled. He also has a nose ring and a slight beard.

Who is this man?

He looks like a grungy, hot supermodel. Not someone who just had his hands around my neck telling me I had one month to pay him back for something I haven't even done.

One of his hands, which is free of tattoos, reaches into his pocket. He pulls out his cell phone, snaps a picture of me, and places it back where it was.

His amber, almond-shaped eyes stare at me as he glances me up and down before speaking, "You look different to Lucy."

My blonde hair doesn't match her black hair. My wide hips don't match her narrow little waist either. If you put us side by side, the only part we got from our mother was her lips, there's not a single thing else. We both look like our fathers—different fathers.

"Do you plan to hurt me?" I ask, managing to look straight into his amber eyes.

"I told you, not yet." His hands stay at his sides, but when I look down, one twitches. I quickly look away and behind me where there is no one.

"They are outside that door." His dark voice rocks through me as I look at the red door that would provide freedom. But what's the use when he knows who I am? He takes a few steps, his lips right at my ear. "You could run. You could definitely make this more fun…"

I turn around fast, and he doesn't step back as he inhales me. My body freezes when a knock on the red door makes him step back just a fraction so he isn't near my neck anymore. A shiver I was holding in wracks through my body.

"One month," he repeats.

"I don't have that kind of money," I reply, looking at him.

"Would you like to make a deal?"

Goddamn! My head tells me no, run, and try to

find a way to make the money. You should never make a deal with a devil. Yet, here I am, nodding my head because my voice is lost.

"I need to hear you say it, Theadora. Would you like to make a deal so you can work off your sister's indiscretions?"

"Yes," I squeak.

He steps forward, his hand reaches up, and when it does, I catch a glimpse of a tattoo from under his black sleeve. Another peeks out from under his collar on his neck. Are they all over his body?

He pulls on a piece of my blonde hair, and then lets it slide between his fingertips.

"I'll own you until her debt is paid. You do understand this?"

Nodding, it seems to be what I am good at right at this moment.

"Your life will not be the same. Any jobs you do for me will be confidential. Do you understand?"

My eyes search around the empty room frantically.

"Theadora, this will not work if you go mute. It will do nothing to assist you, but it will piss me off."

"Yes…" I hiccup. "I understand."

He walks over to a fold-up chair, which is the

only thing in the room, and reaches for a watch, then places it on his wrist.

Why was that off in the first place? is all I can think.

What was he planning to do with me?

"My sister."

"Alive," he says, easing my mind. "For now." Then he walks past, brushing against my arm as he goes to leave me standing in the cold, empty, cement room. He reaches for the red door and pulls it open, letting light in. It's then I see the two guys standing there waiting. Both look at me, then him as he speaks to them before they walk off.

He turns back, those eyes that I'm sure will haunt me tonight stare right at me.

"Goodnight, Theadora Fitzgerald of Thatcher Lane."

My eyes go wide at his words—he knows my street address—before he smirks and turns, letting the red door slam behind him on his way out.

The minute the door shuts I fall to the cold floor, and the tears I have been holding back fall, leaving my soul heavy.

Lucy.

What have you done?

CHAPTER TWO

Atlas

Ocean blue eyes—that's the only reason I didn't kill her, those ocean fucking blue eyes. A woman has never stopped me from doing what I'm meant to be doing. It's how I got to where I am. It's why I am so good at what I do. No one walks over me, and my business thrives on everything I have a hand in.

We sit out front of my building as we wait. The tint on the car windows makes it almost impossible for anyone to see in, and even if she did, Theadora has no idea what car she was put into anyway.

The sun has set when she comes out. The sky

now dark and ominous, which I find fitting. When she emerges with her hands wrapped around her, the skirt she's wearing—which is way too short—seems to be a little higher than it was before. Her lips quiver with the cold, and what fucking beautiful lips they are. She looks down and reachcs for her cell; one of my guys left it there for her so she could get home. I can't have anything happen to her when I have such plans for her.

The minute she stands clutching at her cell, she looks around. It's not a busy area, but there are a number of cars parked along the curb and in a few surrounding lots. I watch as her eyes zoom in on the one we are in. It's as if she can sense me, and it makes me smile. She doesn't move for a moment, simply stares at the car before she looks down at her cell, more than likely getting an Uber.

"Do we wait, sir?" Garry asks.

"Yes," I say without hesitation. "Then follow her."

After she finishes with her cell, she looks back up at our car, her hands skimming at her skirt and her head dropping to the side, assessing where I am. She puts one foot in front of the other toward the car. Is she going to come this way? Maybe even tap on the window? She takes another step in our direction, but she seems to stop herself and puts the cell to her ear. Whoever it is on the other end has distracted her.

"Is she fucking anyone?" I ask Garry, who's been watching her for the last few weeks.

"No sign of any men in her life, sir."

Her eyes look down at her feet as a car pulls around the corner. An Uber must have been close for it to be that fast. Theadora doesn't pull the cell phone away from her ear as she climbs in, but she does look my way one more time.

A smirk I didn't know could form, pushes my lips up.

Those ocean blue eyes are going to be fun to break.

Lucy sits on her bed with her eyes filled with tears.

"Don't tell her. Please, don't tell her."

"She knows, Lucy." My back hits the wall as I watch for her reaction. She doesn't disappoint, taking a deep breath and screaming at me from the bed, but doesn't make a move toward me.

"How could you," Lucy says between hiccups. "How could you?"

"Lucy," I say her name, but she doesn't answer. I take a step toward her, lifting her chin so she has to look at me. There was a time I thought she was beautiful, but now I see the ugly inside her, and that's the way it will be staying. "I could still kill you. Would you prefer I do that instead?"

Lucy is overdramatic, this I have come to realize as we have spent time together. She throws herself back on the bed with her hands above her head as she continues to cry. Her theatrics doing nothing for me.

"She's perfect. Thea is perfect. She already thought I was a bad egg, now you just confirmed it," she says, the tears not leaving.

"Tell me more about Theadora," I ask. Actually, no, it's a command.

Lucy stops the tears straight away and sits upright. Her head drops to the side as she looks at me. "You like her, don't you?"

Lucy doesn't deserve my answers, so I don't say anything.

"She's pretty, but I'm exotic. You can have me! Don't you want me instead?" Lucy's hand touches my arm, and I look down at it.

My tone is aggressive when I speak to her. "Remove your hand, Lucy. Now."

She drops it fast and pulls away from me.

"Tell me about your sister, Lucy. Now."

Her dark eyes, which are the opposite of her

sister's, look at me before she starts talking. And believe me, Lucy likes to talk.

"She manages some shop," she says with an eye roll. "Been working with them since straight out of school." Lucy lies back on her bed and starts to play with her hair, twirling it with her fingers. "She hasn't dated anyone seriously since high school." She pushes up on her arms and looks at me. "Is this what you want to know? Who she's fucking?"

"Who is she fucking?"

"No one. She's a prude with a vicious mouth." She scrunches her nose up. "Thea can be mean with her words." Lucy lies back down and continues to talk while looking at the ceiling. When I get sick of her droning voice, I walk out with ocean blue eyes stuck in my head.

A prude? In that skirt she had on? I don't see that at all.

No, I see her bent over with that skirt around her waist and my hands in her hair as I fuck her from behind.

Shit.

Shaking my shoulders, I get back to work.

CHAPTER THREE

Theadora

I don't go back to work that night to get my car, even though that's where they took me from. I can't seem to get up enough courage to go back there. Not yet. I stay in my small house all night, and the following day I struggle to get up in the afternoon.

Was it a dream? If it was, it was an unbelievably bad dream.

I call Lucy more than once, five times to be precise, and not once does she call me back.

Does he have her? Is she okay?

We may not be the best of friends, but she is my baby sister. And that has to count for something, right? I mean, I agreed to do whatever it was that man wanted from me to protect her.

For fuck's sake, what has she gotten herself into?

Throwing off the covers, I get out of bed and quickly pull on whatever I can find, which consists of gray tracksuit pants that have seen better days and a hoodie that's ten times my size. Putting on my old sneakers and placing my cell in my pocket, I start the trek to Lucy's place. She's living with a friend, and it's not too far from where I live, but we still hardly see each other. Running my hand through my messed-up ponytail, I start to run. She has to be there. If she isn't, then what happened wasn't a dream. Which, right now, I am really hoping it is.

But what about my car?

You left it, so you will have to run. But it doesn't matter, I like running because, for some reason, it calms me.

I slow down when I reach the building where Lucy lives with a roommate. Hers is more open apartments, this one is a block, and Lucy lives on the third floor. There's an elevator that is always broken, so I know I will have to take the stairs.

Kids are out the front kicking a football as I

make my way into her building complex. Glancing at the elevator, the closed sign taped to the front confirms my previous thoughts. Taking the stairs two at a time until I reach the third floor, I walk to her door and notice it's open. Knocking anyway, Mandy ducks her head around and offers me a smile as she stands there with weed in one hand, a lighter in the other.

"Sis." Mandy says with a wave.

I hate when Lucy calls me that—you can guarantee it comes with her wanting something.

"Lucy with you?" Mandy looks past me, then starts to roll the joint in her hand.

"You haven't seen her?"

The joint goes to her lips, and her hair, almost every color of the rainbow, covers her face as she goes to light it. I wonder how often she's set herself on fire, then shake my head at the thought.

Mandy looks up at me, taking a long drag. "Nope, but when you do, tell her rent is overdue. She can't keep expecting me to cover for her."

"You shouldn't cover for her to begin with, Mandy," I say.

Mandy shrugs. "Lucy doesn't have much help. I'm it, you know?"

What a load of shit! Lucy can get anyone to do anything for her. She has that type of charm. She can weave me around her little finger, and I know it. And now look where the fuck that has gotten me. It's also the reason why I'm here. This little visit isn't to see my sister. No, it's to work off her damn debt.

Fucking hell, Lucy! I want to scream the words so loudly, but I hold myself back. Will this sister of mine ever grow the fuck up? She has to. Lucy's twenty-three, and it's time for her to work out what she's going to do with her life.

I'm not her mother.

I'm not even her guardian.

Even if that hurts to say.

I have looked after her for way too long. I cut the strings with her when she reached twenty-one, when she showed me she wasn't planning to do anything but drugs and party for as long as she could.

I won't be an enabler.

I can't because my mother enabled my alcoholic father, and in the end, it's what killed them both.

I will *not* be the same.

"How long has it been since you've seen her, Mandy?"

Mandy, who's clearly forgotten I'm standing at her front door, looks up and smiles. "Ummm…" She scratches her head, and I can see the nicotine marks all over her fingers. "About two weeks or so."

"It's been ten days, to be precise." That dark, menacing voice comes from behind me, and my heart takes a leap in my chest. My hands, which were by my side, reach up to grab the door frame.

"Mandy, do you know this man?"

Mandy, who's way too busy getting high, doesn't even look up, nor does she care by the looks of her.

"No, she doesn't," he answers for her. "I'd prefer to keep it that way. How about you take a walk with me, Theadora, since you're clearly dressed for one."

Removing my hands from the door frame, I manage to turn around to face him. It's slow and awkward, but I need to turn around to make sure he's real.

My eyes stay downcast as his shoes come into focus—black boots. His jeans are rolled up at the bottom—they are ripped and hugging his legs. And as my eyes move farther up, he's wearing a long, white T-shirt.

"Are you working up the nerve to look me in the eye, Theadora?" he teases.

"Yes," I answer truthfully, my eyes sitting at his neckline.

He doesn't move closer, simply reaches his hand

up and goes to touch me. I freeze on the spot as he caresses my cheek ever so softly, and pushes up so I have to look at him. When my eyes meet his, his hand drops, and he wipes his fingers on his jeans, as if touching me was somehow dirty. I don't have any makeup on, so I'm not sure why he felt the need to do that.

"How about we take a walk?" He turns then and starts down the stairs.

Contemplating if I should follow, I wait, just watching him. Looking back over at Mandy, she's now lying on the floor, face toward the ceiling with her eyes closed.

"Theadora." My name comes impatiently from his lips.

"Do you have her? Answer me, and I will follow. Do you have Lucy with you?" I yell. I can't see him anymore, so it means he's already down the first flight of stairs.

"Yes, I have her. You know this."

Something inside of me deflates as I close my eyes. I put one foot in front of the other and walk to the stairs. Touching the railing, I feel its cold metal between my fingertips and look down. He's there, standing halfway down the next flight of stairs, looking up, watching me with his hands at his sides, his mouth in a straight line, and those eyes locked onto me. Does he know what emotion is?

Stepping down the stairs quickly, I come up behind him, stopping until he starts to move again. I can smell him. The scent is of smoked wood and the ocean, and I think, *How is that even possible?*

When we reach the bottom, he holds the door open for me, letting me walk out first. The sun hits my face as it starts to set. Turning back to look at him, he's watching me, eyeing me up and down, which makes me feel like I shouldn't have left the house in what I'm wearing in the first place.

"You dress like this normally?"

Ignoring his words, because he does not need an answer as to how I dress, I walk past him until I am on the side of the road to head back toward my place. I pause, thinking if that's a smart idea, then realize he has been there before. He knows where I live, and probably a whole lot more than he's letting me believe.

"You're wondering if you should go toward your house, but then you realized I know exactly where you live."

My head flicks back to him, fast.

"Am I wrong? I am hardly ever wrong." His mouth moves, but there's hardly any real movement. There's no emotion; everything he says is dry and lifeless. He steps in front of me until he reaches a car that is similar to the one my boss owns. I know it's expensive because when she purchased it, the first thing she did was bring it out and show it off. Then she told us the price tag; it was more than what I could make in years of working.

He opens the passenger door, then looks at me, his eyes on my baggy clothes before he waves to his door. "Let me take you to get your car, which I know you haven't collected from your work."

"What is your name?" I ask, realizing he's never given it to me.

Oh, Thea, when was he meant to give it to you? When he kidnapped you?

I shake my head at his open door and his non-answer of my question.

So, he can know everything about me, but I am not allowed to know anything about him?

"Get in the car, Theadora, we have things to discuss."

"You won't hurt me?" I touch my forehead where a bruise is still forming from when he took me.

His gaze skims over the spot, then focuses back on my eyes. "No. I will not touch you at all."

I believe him. I don't know why, but for some reason, I do.

Walking over to his car, where he's already standing, I climb inside, and he shuts the door behind me. Looking forward, I see the car is even flashier inside than my boss's and think that maybe this is an upgraded model.

"You don't plan to kidnap me again?" I ask while buckling my seatbelt.

"Not today," he says, pushing the button to start it. He heads off in the direction of where I work. At first, no other words are spoken, and my leg starts to involuntarily bounce as I wait. He can't seriously offer me a lift and demand I get in the car with him if he doesn't plan to speak to me. What's the point?

"You seem agitated. Do you get agitated a lot?" he asks with his hands firmly on the wheel, staring ahead.

"Just when I'm in a car with a kidnapper," I retort while scrunching up my nose, but with a smile.

He huffs as if he finds my words amusing. "Maybe you should take better care of your family."

Oh no, he didn't just say that! He has some cheek, I will give him that. Take better care of my family? Who the fuck does he think he is? All I have ever done is take care of Lucy. In the end it got tiring, and I couldn't keep doing it. The fact it was bringing me down as well meant I needed to allow her to stand on her own two feet. She is an adult, and it was time for her to grow up.

"You know fuck all. Keep your damn words to yourself, unless you plan to use them in a way you know is true." My hands clutch together, and I sit there waiting for him to tell me off, to tell me he's planning to punish me for the way I've just spoken to him. Anything. But he does nothing but drive in silence until my blue car comes into view parked exactly where I left it.

Guess he didn't want to talk after all.

When he comes to a stop, he clicks the doors unlocked and stares straight ahead. "You'll accompany me tomorrow night to a function. Your payments start then," he growls with his fists clenched and eyebrows firmly pinched together in a scowl.

I know there's no room for me to argue. I am to go to whatever function he wants me to and do as he asks, it's part of the deal.

"Dress?" I ask, in a voice that I hope isn't shaky. I don't want to give him anything.

"Cocktail. Something will be sent to your house in the morning."

"I have work."

"It will be there before you leave." He dismisses me.

I slide out of his car and head to mine, and when I turn back, he's watching me. But I can't make out his expression.

And that?

That's what scares me.

CHAPTER FOUR

Theadora

My hands freeze in my hair as I'm tying my locks up into a messy bun, due to a knock on my front door that comes hard and fast. Taking a deep breath, I quickly finish tying it up and walk with steady steps to my front door. Another knock, louder this time, comes before I get there. Whoever it is, they're impatient. Touching the door, I pull it open, but standing there is a girl with glasses on her face, black hair tied back into a tight ponytail, her lips painted red, and dressed in a black dress shirt and pencil skirt. I have never seen this woman before in my life, but the way she is looking at me makes me believe instantly that she dislikes me.

"Theadora," she snaps.

"Thea," I correct her.

"Yes, well, here is your dress. Be ready by six sharp. The car will be here to collect you." She pushes the dress into my hands and turns, walking away while I watch. As she reaches a waiting black car, she turns back. "Don't be late. He hates tardiness." Then she climbs in and drives off.

I look down at the dress in my hands, which is covered in a bag reading Gucci. Closing the front door, I take it to my couch and lay it down, unzipping the bag. At first, I'm shocked. I've seen this dress online—it's part of what I do, hunt for outfits and what is popular. This dress is one of the popular ones, and it was one of the first to come up in my search. This dress is also over four thousand dollars.

Holding it up in front of me, I admire the beautiful garment. It has slim shoulder straps. One side is gold and falls just to the knee, while the other side is black and sits higher on the upper thigh. It has rumpled fabric where the gold and black meet in the midsection.

Placing the dress back down, I shake my head and step away from it. He would have rented it.

High-end clothing stores do that now, let you hire expensive dresses for a night so you can show off, then return them the next day. Our boss has been looking at doing something similar.

Grabbing my purse, I look back one more time at the dress.

Who is this man?

And what am I expected to do tonight that requires me to wear a dress that costs so much?

I'm late. Dammit! I can't help it because work ran over. Our computer system crashed, which left us manually entering orders and hoping and praying we have the stock to cover it.

Arriving at my house at quarter to six, there's a limousine sitting out the front. Grabbing my bag out of the car, I run past it and up the few stairs until I reach my front door.

"Theadora." He inflects the last part of my name, making me feel like a naughty schoolgirl. "My assistant would have told you I hate tardiness. Yet, here you are, not even dressed." I turn at the sound of his voice and see him standing at the limousine door, holding it open with one arm. He's dressed in a black suit, and instead of a white undershirt, it's black. It makes his amber eyes appear even darker.

"I'll be ready in fifteen minutes," I tell him.

He looks to his watch and frowns.

I don't waste any more time as I run inside and start tearing off my clothes and going straight to that dress. It's already laid out on my couch, so once I am naked, I slide it on over my body. A dress like this, that's body-hugging and fits perfectly, does not require me to wear a bra, which might show straps, or even underwear, which will show lines. No, this dress requires nothing but a pair of heels. I borrowed a pair from work that are gold, matching the color of half of the dress. Untying my hair, I let it fall and twist half of it into a loose bun, pulling strands around my face to give it a waterfall effect before I switch to a black bag and walk toward the door. When I open it exactly fifteen minutes later, right at six o'clock, he looks up at me in surprise, as if he wasn't expecting me to be ready.

"Will you give me your name now? Or what shall I call you at this event?"

"You aren't at this event to impress me. I want you to make my guys spend." He holds open the limousine door, waving a hand impatiently for me to get in. When he slides in, he glowers, and I wonder what on earth has him so angry at me now. I am on time, just like he asked me to be.

"So, you're like my pimp? You dress me and tell me what guys I should talk to?" I ask while screwing up my face.

As the limousine takes off, his hands come to his lap, and I watch as he screws them up in balls clenched so hard that they are turning red then white.

"It's best you stay quiet," he says, looking out the window.

What the hell ever! I huff and reach for my cell and lipstick. It's the only thing I didn't have time to apply. Turning on my camera so I can see, I apply it, turning my pale pink lips more of a blush color. Wiping the edges, I put both my cell and lipstick away, and when I do, I feel his gaze hard on me.

He asked me not to speak, so not speaking is what I will be doing.

My cell dings, and I smile at my co-worker's message. It's a picture of her eyes wide and a big fat smile on her face, with a caption that reads, 'Computers are working again.'

Typing back a smiley face, I send her a selfie along with a thumbs up. Hitting send, I turn to see amber eyes trained on me. Remembering he doesn't want me to speak, I raise an eyebrow at him.

With amused eyes, he studies me before the car comes to a stop and my door is opened for me. A hand is offered, but I don't take it. For all I know, that hand could have been one of the ones that grabbed me to begin with. Touching my forehead where I know the bruise is located, I shake my head and stand waiting for *him* to get out.

A voice comes from behind me and says, "Atlas," and nothing more. My eyebrows pinch together as I turn to look at him while he smooths out the wrinkles in his suit and does up the button on his jacket. With his lips in a thin line, he walks past me, leaving me standing there confused by his single word.

He turns back, noticing I haven't moved, and offers me his elbow. "The name is Atlas." His lips turn up in a wry smile. "But you can call me, sir, along with everyone else."

I walk up to him and look at his offered elbow, then head off straight ahead, not taking it. "Shall we?"

He drops his arm and walks alongside me into the venue, which I know to be a local casino.

"She worked for you, didn't she?" I ask in a hushed breath.

"She did," Atlas answers truthfully.

I know because when Lucy got this job, she was

excited and told me all about it. I had hopes she was getting on the straight and narrow. I guess I was wrong, and it seems about a lot of things lately.

"Sir, the room is ready, and players are set up." A security guard stands in front of us.

Atlas looks down at me. "Push your tits up more." He eyes them. "What you have anyway." His nose scrunches up. "You have men to distract." Then he's gone, and I'm left standing with the security guard who looks down at my cleavage, then turns away.

Did that bastard just insult my tits?

"Follow me," the security guard says.

My hands cup my breasts, and I do as he says, pushing them up as we walk through a door that leads to a kitchen, then through yet another door, which, once it's opened, allows the sounds of music and laughter to drift through.

"That man is on Australia's most wanted list, and he is our highest bidder tonight. Distract him enough to make sure he loses. Do whatever you need to. What he loses will be taken off your debt, so make it count," the security guard states, then steps back out the door, shutting it behind him.

My hands clutch my purse with determination. If he is a big bidder, that means if I make him lose at least half of his winnings, it could be a huge chunk off what Lucy owes.

Eyeing him up and down, I notice he is round, very round. Everywhere. Wondering why he is wanted by authorities probably isn't a smart move; I am better off not knowing. Looking around, there are another five men in the room totaling six, with two waitresses, and one other girl dressed like I am smiling at one man in particular, which isn't the man I need to impress, thank God.

Walking to the bar where he's seated, chips in hand, I tap the bar with my fingers as the bartender walks over.

"What can I get ya?"

"Just water, thanks."

The bartender squints, then pours a glass of water, making it fancy with a few blocks of ice and a lemon wedge, then he leaves it on the counter before he walks away.

"Water? What's your real motive?"

I turn, managing to keep my face smiling as I look at him. His hair, likely once dark, is faded and receding, brushed over to compensate for the loss of fullness. I look down to the floor and back to him, hoping my eyes portray innocence. Men love it when a woman is naive. It brings their macho genes into play, and they get to be the gods they think they are.

"My sister convinced me to come... said it would be thrilling," I tell him with a bite of my bottom lip. I lean in closer. "Is it? Thrilling?"

He smirks as if he's won the damn lottery. "It sure is, babe. Stick with me, and I'll show you a good time."

I brush him off. "I don't want to be a pain. I mean... I don't even know how to play."

"You don't need to know how to play, you just need to watch."

I nod as he calls the bartender over. "Now, tell him what you really want to drink."

"Vodka," I reply.

The bartender nods and pours me a straight vodka over ice and hands it to me, which makes the man next to me smile.

"That's more like it."

I take a sip, and when I do, I realize it's exactly what I had before. *Water.*

Looking up at the bartender, he taps his ear, then points to the camera above the bar.

Of course I can't drink, because that would make it easier.

Round man, which is what I have decided to call him, touches my bare leg, and I have to remember to not throw him off and slap him for touching me.

"Stay close, babe, you may just be my good luck charm."

Yeah, fucking right.

Everyone walks over to the tables and takes their seats. The round man makes sure I am right next to him as he starts playing. He begins with one thousand dollars, and I have to remember to keep my lips from opening and saying something at his disrespect for spending so much money on gambling. That money could be used on so many good things instead of going to a man who's most definitely an asshole.

He plays his first hand, and I don't do much of anything. Round man drinks four drinks while he plays, and by his fifth his arm reaches out and wraps around my waist.

Distract.

Deflect.

Sidetrack him.

I look past round man to where I know the camera is located and glance up at it before I let my lips touch the round man's neck while whispering to him asking if he needs a drink. But in reality it's a distraction method.

It works, and he keeps me glued to him, not

caring that he has already lost fifty-thousand dollars by the end of the first hand.

"Gentlemen." I giggle as round man touches my leg again, this time taking it up higher over my dress but now on my thigh, as I look up to the voice that has entered the room.

I could pick that voice out of a line-up.

Atlas walks over to me, nods to round man, then sits in the spare seat next to me. Round man's hand pauses on my leg as the game continues. He seems to be paying more attention, and he adds another fifty thousand dollars, which ups his bet to one hundred and fifty.

I touch his shoulder, stroking it gently as it comes around to his turn. He loses again, and instead of being angry, he turns to kiss me. I manage to move my head at the very last second, making his lips touch my cheek. When I do move my face, I see Atlas, who's watching me with amusement and fascination in his eyes.

Someone wins.

The game is done.

I go to peel myself from round man, but he holds on tight.

"I would gladly lose again, double that amount, if it means I get to take you home for the night."

My eyes go wide at his words.

What? I did not agree to that.

I am no man's whore.

Scanning around the room, I find Atlas talking to another player when our eyes connect.

He smirks, then turns and walks away.

CHAPTER FIVE

Atlas

I watched her play the perfect part. Theadora did exactly as I thought she would and was the perfect distraction. Lucy once did the same, but Lucy liked to play with the big boys, and she tended to push buttons to see how far she could go, which wasn't all that wise.

Theadora, well, she is the complete opposite of her sister in every way possible.

Which makes her interesting.

Lucy is like the grass that's always green in winter—predictable and simple.

Theadora is like the thorns that sting when you

touch a beautiful rose—multidimensional and complex.

She is riveting.

I like to watch her.

I want to study her.

See what makes her tick. Is it me or is it something else?

"Remove Mr. London and escort Theadora home."

"He will *not* be happy," Garry says with a smirk.

"No. No, he probably won't be." I wouldn't be happy either if someone was about to pull Theadora out of my bed. But the difference between Mr. London and me, she would never dare enter my bed, nor will she be allowed near it. "And tell her to keep the dress."

Garry nods and walks off.

I go back to the office and turn on the camera so I can see her—she's looking up at it for help. And as if she knows it's me watching her, she raises her middle finger so no one else can see and flips me off.

I smile. A big, fat smile.

I haven't done that in a long time.

Garry walks over to her, and she turns away from the camera. He speaks to Mr. London, who does not look pleased that he's being told he's about to lose his blonde beauty, and Theadora is replaced with a call girl who I have on staff who is more than happy to have sex for money. She touches him where he wants to be touched, soothing his outburst that was about to come, with her warm hands in just the right places.

Theadora looks up to the camera as she is walking out and her lips thin before I can no longer see her.

"Just over two hundred thousand," our accounts guy tells me. "Seems she may be a lucky charm," he states, then turns, leaving my office.

Her player lost almost all of his hands, which with what her sister owes, is a significant amount to pay back. Mr. London only loses when he's distracted. If you take away the womanly distractions, he will always win. But put them in his way, and we will win. We learned this earlier when he first started coming into the casino.

As I start to close everything down for the evening, in walks Sydney with a clipboard in hand and glasses on.

"Lucy is screaming for attention, and her sister seems to be asking Garry for information on you," she says, looking up over the rim of her glasses.

"Give Lucy what she wants, and who cares, let Theadora dig. He won't say anything."

Sydney nods then turns to leave. "Should I collect the dress tomorrow?"

"No," I say, looking up at Sydney.

"That's a four-thousand-dollar dress, sir. Do you plan to make her pay that back too, or let her keep it to sell?"

"Does it matter to you, Sydney, what she does with it?"

Sydney wrinkles her nose. "No. Not at all. Goodnight, sir." She walks out, shutting the door behind her.

I didn't intend for Theadora to keep that dress, that was until I saw it on her. What kind of woman gets ready in fifteen minutes and walks out looking like she spent many hours on herself when I know damn well she didn't?

A vixen, that's what she is.

I've seen her dress down, and now I have seen her dress up. And I know what she likes. I may not know all her qualities, but I am sure she's not like most other women.

Theadora has a temper, she's feisty, and her eyes look at me as if she's trying to work out my best-kept secrets. Well, unlucky for her, no one knows my secrets. Sometimes I wonder if even I do.

But I plan to keep it that way.

A devil doesn't show his hand. He plays his cards until the winning hand is revealed.

I think she may be my favorite playing card yet.

And I plan to play every move possible when it comes to her.

CHAPTER SIX

Theadora

"Keep the dress." That's what the driver guy said before he drove off.

Surely, Atlas should know I would try to sell the dress so I can add it to the money to pay him back and have him out of my life faster. So, I put the dress up for sale today for half the price, and the minute it was online my cell phone rang.

"Hello."

"Selling that dress will not help you. It's not your money I will accept as payment, Theadora. It's a waste of time." Atlas voice rings through, then he hangs up without another word.

Fuck!

How on earth could he have possibly known I placed it online for sale? And so quickly too.

Huffing, I took the post down. There was no point in selling it if he wouldn't take my money.

Shit. I wonder what else he will make me do.

I am back at the office today, and Michelle asks me as she walks past, "Hey, it's Marissa's birthday Friday night. You still planning to come?"

Anything will be better than the last weekend I had.

"Yep."

"Awesome. Marissa is bringing her brother. She said she plans to set you up, so word of warning." Michelle smiles before ducking off.

Oh, for fuck's sake, that's the last thing I need right now—a man in my life—especially with everything I have going on.

I don't even know when Atlas will call me. I haven't seen him since Monday night, and apart from today's call to tell me to pull the dress down, I don't know his plans beyond that. Honestly, he can ask whatever. He could make me be a stripper at Marissa's birthday party and I would say yes because I need him gone and for my sister to be safe.

My head tells me he isn't that dangerous, but

then I look at the fading bruise on my forehead and know otherwise.

He kidnapped me.

He could have killed me or done worse.

Even if he looks at me as if he's trying to work me out, Atlas is anything but kind.

He's silent.

Deadly.

Ruthless.

And way too handsome for his own good. Which is probably the reason women overlook his evil tendencies. Well, I have seen glimpses, and I know better than to trust him or believe he won't kill me when he has no more use for me.

I was living in a world where evil wasn't part of my life. I believed that even bad people could be good if you looked inside them hard enough.

What am I? Snow White?

Perhaps I'm wrong.

Maybe bad is bad.

And there's no fixing that kind of evil.

"Well, holy shit, woman," Marissa says as she walks into my office holding an exceptionally large vase of flowers.

Looking up, I reach for them and take the card attached. Turning it over, I see no writing, only the letter 'A.'

Is he playing games with me now?

"Are you seeing someone? Please tell me you aren't?"

Oh, that's right, her brother.

"Yes," I lie. The last thing I need right now is a blind date I didn't agree on.

"Oh, dang. Really?"

"Really." I smile. I hate that I'm lying to her, but I do it anyway.

"Okay, well bring him Friday, I would love to meet him." Marissa places the flowers down on the desk. "I mean, he sure as shit does have great taste in flowers… and women." She winks before walking out.

Hell no. That will never happen. I don't know a single person who starts with the letter 'A' apart from Atlas, and the last thing I want to do is accept gifts from that man.

Picking the flowers up, I place them in the trash can and get back to work.

Fuck you, Atlas!

And fuck your damn flowers.

A bunch of flowers is delivered every day until Friday, and each time I throw them in the trash.

Friday's flowers I will take to Marissa for her birthday, as she will get way more joy out of them than the trash will.

Getting dressed that night to have some drinks, the Gucci dress sits in my cupboard taunting me. I should burn it. But why would I do that to such a wonderful piece of material? It's made of silk from Italy. That dress is a masterpiece, and burning it may hurt my soul.

Calling a cab, I go straight to the bar where Marissa is celebrating. When I walk in, I see her table near the bar decorated with pink balloons. She's wearing a bright pink dress, and she looks beautiful. All the girls from work are here, and there are also a few faces I don't know.

"Thea, this is Sebastian, my brother."

He stands to greet me. Sebastian's tall, maybe taller than Atlas's six-two.

Fuck! Why on earth did I just compare them?

Atlas is the devil reincarnated.

Sebastian's hair is the same color as Marissa's chocolate brown and their smiles almost match.

"I've heard a lot about you," he says with a smile. He reaches out and grips onto my hand. The music isn't too loud here at the back, but the dance floor at the front is almost filled at ten at night.

"All good, I hope?"

Sebastian nods slowly, letting go of my hand. He is damn good looking. Even my type, if I had a type. When he smiles, I know he means it—it's not fake nor forced. And better yet, he smiles at me.

"You two could have had such pretty babies," Marissa says, leaning her head on mine as I look up at Sebastian with wide eyes and raised eyebrows.

"She talks about you a lot," he says, then smirks. "Don't worry, soon her boyfriend will be here, and she can talk babies with him." Sebastian winks at me, easing my nerves while I take a seat next to Marissa.

"Dean doesn't want to talk babies," Marissa says, taking a large sip from her straw. "We are too young," she continues with an eye roll.

"You are. Just have fun," Sebastian says.

Marissa has just turned twenty-one, and she said her brother is five years older than her, so he's my age.

"I'm maternal, what can I say?" Marissa throws up a hand, holding her drink in the other but almost spilling it while she does. "It's nice of you to come. Did you invite your boyfriend? I would looovvveee...." she slurs, leaning into me, "... to meet him."

"No." Because I don't have one, but she doesn't need to know that.

"Whyyy?"

The waiter brings another round of drinks, and I take one. I don't plan to stay long. My mind is preoccupied and worried about my sister. Is Lucy all right? If I take Atlas's word for it, she is, but I won't rest easy until I can see her with my own two eyes. And right now, I don't really know if she's okay or not.

"Let's leave your boss alone and grill her another time. Why don't you go and dance?" Sebastian says, nodding to Marissa's other friends out on the dance floor already. She listens, standing and walking off to the dance floor.

"She's been trying to set us up for quite some time now," Sebastian tells me, which pulls me from my raging thoughts.

I smile up at him. "I've only just heard about it."

"I figured as much. She likes to do that. Surprise people with things she likes to control," he says.

I look past him to the dance floor and watch Marissa dancing for a short time, then say, "I should go. I have a busy weekend planned, and she is well on her way to having a great evening anyway. Will you tell her goodnight for me?" I ask while standing and placing my drink down.

"It's not anything I said, is it?"

"Oh no, not at all. I just have a lot on my plate, and the last thing I need is to be staying out all night drinking." I smile and walk past him to the front. As I reach for the door, hands wrap around my arm, stopping me from going any farther. I'm about to scream and punch whoever touched me when I turn and see Atlas's amber eyes, which freeze me into position.

"Interesting finding you here." His dark eyes don't leave mine, and my pulse races at his touch.

I try to pull free, but he doesn't loosen his grip. People walking past look, but no one says a word.

"Maybe you are a lot like your sister. After all, this was where I found her spending my money," he says with venom in his tone.

Licking my lips because they're dry, his eyes drop to them and watch the movement. I can feel my cheeks heating at his glaring eyes.

"Let go of my arm before I knee you between your legs." I spit out his name, "*Atlas*."

He shows me his teeth, as if he's going to bite me, then releases my arm. When he does, I take a step back so our bodies no longer touch.

"Your sister did the opposite… she threw herself at me." There's a smirk, a pause, then he continues, "Where you want to maim me."

"If I could, I would never see your face again." I smile as I say those words because they please me. Turning, now that I am free of his hold, I walk out of the club and wave down a cab. Atlas follows me outside and stands next to me, his team of security, or whatever the hell they are, all stand back. I didn't even notice they were there with him when he had his hands on me.

"Are you following me?" I swing my head around to look at him. His hands are in the pockets of his black trousers.

"No, you're in one of my establishments. Coincidence only."

"Yeah, sure… if *you* want to call it that." My words are clipped, and I am angry.

"You have a mouth on you, that's for sure. The last woman who spoke to me that way ended up with my cock in her mouth to shut her up," he declares smugly.

I gasp, my cheeks reddening at the thought. "That will never happen. You will never happen." I shiver at the thought, showing my disgust outwardly.

"You try to be a good liar, but you suck at it. Bad." His voice turns smooth, and I have to look away or he will know I am just that, a liar. Even if there are some parts of me that are disgusted by him. Actually, no, a lot of me is disgusted by him, but I still think he is incredibly attractive. I am not blind to his outward charm.

"I feel like you wouldn't really be able to recognize a liar from someone telling the truth. Everyone in your circle probably lies to you anyway, or maybe they just tell you what you want to hear." The cab pulls up, and I open the door, looking back to him. "Goodnight, Atlas, enjoy your evening." I climb in and try not to look back as the driver drives off. My cell dings, and I pull it out to read the message.

Unknown: Only someone with a death wish lies to me. Would you be so stupid?

I save his number and choose not to reply. I feel like Atlas is a man who's used to getting what he wants, and he simply doesn't care who he hurts to achieve his goals.

I am not that person.

I choose to *not* be his new plaything.

CHAPTER SEVEN

Theadora

His secretary is at my door again, this time with another new dress. This is twice this week. Will I be doing the same thing? I feel even if I ask the question, I won't get the answer from her anyway. Her whole face seems to be in a permanent scowl.

"He told me to tell you to be ready by eight. Atlas said that should be plenty of time from now. You're to wear the heels you had on last night…" she pushes the dress bag into my hands, "… with this."

"Umm… okay. Anything else?"

"Your sister is a cunt! Thought you should know that," she asserts with a scowl and slight drop of her head.

My eyes go wide at her words. "You've seen her. She's okay?"

"He told you she was okay, so, of course, she is."

"Yes, but I haven't seen proof. Am I just meant to take the word of a man who is blackmailing me?" I ask, pointing out the damn obvious.

"He could have killed you. It's been done before. So, yes, you should take the word from a man who's looking after your sister instead of killing the both of you." She turns and walks out my door.

I follow and stand on the step. "You don't like me. Why?" I question her.

She looks up over her glasses. "Because you hold a power I don't possess." Then she climbs in her car, slams the door, and drives off the same as last time.

Going inside, with the dress still in hand, I notice this one reads, Saint Laurent. Fucking hell! Why does he keep sending me expensive dresses to wear? I am not keeping this one, no fucking way. Upon opening the zipper, I see the bright pink foil-looking dress. This one is short, cute but very short. It has a one-shoulder neckline and a shimmering look about it.

In a word or two—it's fucking beautiful.

And the same price tag as the last one.

Sliding it on, I start to get ready. This time I actually take longer than fifteen minutes, since I have more time. I curl my hair and loosely pile it on top of my head, securing it with bobby pins. Then grabbing my black heels I had on last night, I put them on, then finish my makeup. I take my time adding a bright pink lip-gloss to match the dress, and shimmery pink and smoky eyelids.

Fifteen minutes to eight, I hear a knock on my door. Is he early? Grabbing my purse, I go to open the door, and as I do, another knock comes. Pulling it open, Atlas is standing there, hand raised as he looks at me.

"You assumed I would be late?" I ask him, my hand going to my hip.

Devilish eyes assess me. "No. You do not disappoint." He turns, walks to the car, and holds open the door for me.

"What am I to be doing tonight? Flirting with the round man again?" I question with an eye roll.

"Round man?"

"Yes. He is round and loud," I reply while sliding into the car.

"Mr. London is…" He thinks on it while sliding in after me, then he fixes his suit jacket, which is much the same as the last time. "I guess, yes, he is round," he states with a head nod. "But, no, tonight you will observe and listen for me. Don't speak to anyone, do not tell anyone who you are with or your name. Do you understand?"

I nod at his request.

"I need to hear you say it, Theadora. Speak that you understand. It's paramount that you do. These men are dangerous."

"I'm in a car with one, am I not?" I say, referring to someone who's fucking dangerous.

"Touché. Now, tell me you understand. That you will be quiet and not speak. Just listen."

"What am I listening for exactly?"

"If you hear my name or my casino's name, that's what you should be listening out for."

"Okay, I think I can do that."

"Think?" He raises an eyebrow.

"I can do that." I nod. "Is this the stuff you had Lucy doing?" I brave a question in the hopes he will answer.

"You want to discuss your sister?" he asks, to which I nod my head eagerly.

"That can be arranged once you pay off her debt."

The car comes to a stop and Atlas opens his door.

"The car will take you around the block one more time. Your name will be at the door for entry."

"I can't come in with you?" I ask.

"No. Now you know what you are to do?"

"Listen," I say.

"Yes. Listen and don't talk to anyone, Theadora."

"How much will this knock off? I calculated the other night I have worked, and you said it was over a million. So how much does tonight equate to?" I ask, hoping for some kind of answer.

"We will discuss upon your completion tonight."

I nod.

Atlas shuts the door, and the car takes off around the block. I check my cell purely out of nervousness and put it straight back in my purse. When we reach the front again, I climb out and walk the steps until I arrive at the person who's holding an iPad checking names. Giving them my name, they smile, then let me inside.

I enter by myself, while almost everyone else in here is standing with someone or holding someone's hand.

"Can I get you a drink?"

I smile and shake my head, and the waiter walks away. Walking around, I spot Atlas straight away.

He isn't hard to miss. I think almost every woman here has ogled him at some point. Even the wife whose husband Atlas is talking with is looking at him as if he's her next meal, even as she stands there holding her husband's arm.

I look away from his perfectly crafted hair and nose ring that makes him look even more appealing. Reaching in my bag for my AirPods, I place them in my ears with my phone in hand and walk to a small empty table situated behind a few guys who are bundled around another table talking.

"Yes, I know what you mean, but explain it again," I say to my phone with my AirPods in my ears as I feel eyes on me. Of course, I have loosely placed the AirPods so I can still hear everything being said. Most people will go about their conversations if they think you're preoccupied.

Which is exactly what they do.

"He came alone," one man says.

"He's never alone. Don't fool yourself. He didn't get where he is at his age being foolish. Now go and introduce yourself before he moves to the next, and take that piece of ass with you, so she can pry her way into his bed."

I look to my side and see one man walk away with a woman attached to his arm. Not too far in front of them is Atlas. He's holding a drink in hand while he nods his head to what someone's saying. I watch as the man with the woman walks up to him, then watch in fascination as the woman does exactly what she was asked to do, stands next to Atlas and turns on her charm.

Is she like me? Being blackmailed into doing things we don't want to? It's the only explanation I can give myself for why this woman is listening to men to sell herself to.

Atlas's eyes flick to me, and my cell buzzes in my hand.

Atlas: What did you hear?

His name comes up as I read the message. Looking away from him, I type out my reply and watch as he reads it.

Me: She's to find a way to sleep with you.

His lips move as if he's fighting a smirk while he glances at the man who's in front of him. The man laughs at something Atlas says, but Atlas makes no movement to indicate he cares for what this man has to say. Atlas places an arm around the woman, leans down and whispers in her ear, and while he does, his eyes search for mine, locking on as he whispers to her, then looks away. My breath, which I didn't realize I was holding, escapes, and I make a move to the bar. The waiter comes over, and I order a glass of champagne—one glass can't hurt, and I really need it right now to calm my nerves.

Turning around with the glass in hand, I almost spill it as I bump into Atlas, who's there in front of me. He takes the glass from my hand and walks back to where he was previously standing.

What the actual fuck?

"Well, didn't see that one coming," a voice comes from next to me.

Turning, I come face to face with a man who's dressed to kill. He looks good, really good. The man almost rivals Atlas with his looks, but there's something about Atlas that makes him stand out from the rest.

The man picks up a handful of peanuts and throws one into his mouth, closing his lips to chew. He has full lips and high cheekbones. His light-colored hair is a contrast to his tanned skin and playful smile. He almost looks like he's walked out of a surfing competition and threw on a suit.

Choosing to ignore him, I turn around and order a water instead. This time when I turn around, no one is there to take it from me.

Fuck! I really do need a drink now.

"So, you're his new plaything." Turning back to that voice, another peanut is popped into his mouth. He throws the next one high in the air and catches it. When I don't answer, he smirks. "My guess is he told you not to talk. Smart move." He nods, then looks at where Atlas is standing. I follow his line of sight and watch as Atlas walks away with that woman, his hand on her hip as they disappear out of sight.

I look to the stranger who seems to know more than he should, and offer him a smile before I place my water down and go to where I saw Atlas leave.

"I wouldn't do that if I were you." I look back, and the stranger smiles. "Name's Benji, sweetheart." I don't give him my name. Instead, I simply offer a small smile before I continue to follow Atlas.

As I reach the door I saw him walk out of, I push it just a fraction and freeze as I hear sounds, very familiar sounds.

Grunts and groans of pleasure.

Pushing the door just a little bit farther, I see him, his back against the wall with that woman down on her knees as she strokes his cock with her hand, her red lips wrapped around the top.

I should walk away.

I should back away slowly, so he doesn't know what I've just seen, but as I look up, I see him smirking as if he knew I would follow.

My eyes go wide as the girl tries to take more of him in her mouth, but she can't because he's so big.

My eyes flick back up to him, and his hand is now in her hair, gripping it as he shows her exactly what to do—what he likes.

As he closes his eyes, enjoying the moment, I back away, letting the door close.

And I wonder if I run, will he catch me?

CHAPTER EIGHT

Atlas

I get off when people think they can fuck with me, that they can have what's mine, and try to take it from my greedy hands.

That, of course, is impossible and will never happen.

Once I lay claim to something, I do not let it go. It's why I have not taken a woman longer than a few nights. I would swallow a woman whole, and she wouldn't be able to escape me. That's what type of love mine would be—all-encompassing—and I know this, so I stay away.

The girl between my legs comes up for air, licks her pink lips, and tries to lift my shirt.

That is not going to happen.

Pushing her hands away, I tuck myself back into my pants and straighten my suit.

She gets off her knees and pulls her dress down. "You don't want to fuck? We could go back to yours and do what you want... *all night*," she sing-songs the last two words.

"No. Go back to Harry and tell him your services have been fulfilled."

Her face drops, and she looks down at the floor.

"It's not like that," she says.

"It is. And sweetheart? You can do better." I give her my card and walk out the door, the same one Theadora slipped out of. She's easy to spot, standing out like a rose in the middle of thorns. In her hand is a glass of water, and I want to smile that she listened to me.

"My man." Someone taps on my back.

I turn to see Benji and shrug him off, to which he offers me a smile.

"She's a looker, that one. You pick her?" His eyes find Theadora and then switch back to me. "What am I saying... of course you did. You would have had her under watch for at least a few weeks." He pins me with his eyes. "Or shorter maybe, considering how controlling of her you are already."

"She's a pawn in a game. Nothing more."

"I'm sure she is. So you wouldn't mind if I went over there and introduced myself, would you?" Benji straightens his tie and smirks.

"Do as you please," I say through gritted teeth, looking away from her.

Benji eyes me before he nods. "Okay then," he states before he takes off in Theadora's direction. She offers him a smile when he sits next to her, and I watch while Benji talks to her. She doesn't speak back, only nods and looks around the room.

"Do you want me to break that up?" Garry asks, standing beside me, nodding toward Benji.

"No. Let's see how loyal she is in helping her sister."

"She can't do her job from over there," he says, pointing out the obvious.

I turn to him.

He looks down. "Sorry, sir." And he backs away.

"You told my gift she can do better?" Harry questions me while shaking his head. Normal people would be afraid of Harry. Lucky for me, I am not normal.

I was raised by one of the most ruthless men, who made no excuses for his actions, and if you stepped out of line you were beaten into submission.

My father was a criminal in almost every aspect. My mother ran away when I was a year old, and I have no memory of her. But him? Him I can never escape, even if he is behind bars for the rest of his life. Being raised by that man made me stronger, made me learn from his mistakes, and made me realize I will never be like him.

My hands don't touch women unless in the throes of pleasure, and believe me, my hands around Theodora's throat tested my every resolve. I want to fuck her hard and grip her sweet, soft neck when I do.

I have rules, though. And I feel she may break every single one of them if I let her close.

1. Do not fall in love.
2. Never let women dictate who you are. They will bring you down and crush you while taking your money.
3. Business above all else.
4. My gun doesn't aim unless you betray me.

And I'm really hoping Theadora doesn't betray me. Because a bullet in that perfect head could really mess up that gorgeous hair. And we wouldn't want that now, would we.

Turning back to Harry, I can see he's angry. He runs one of the most expensive and exclusive whorehouses in town. The asshole sells his women for a few hours and only gives them a fraction of what he makes.

So yes, she can do better.

Much, much better than Harry's whorehouse.

"You think you are so much better than us, don't you? Why? Because you own that casino?" he huffs.

Yes, yes, I do. My casino started off small, but now it's one of the biggest in the state and attracts all kinds of patrons. It has rooms that can only be accessed if you know me personally, and I don't like many people, so access to those rooms is very exclusive.

My private bar area costs over one hundred thousand dollars for rental, and that's the starting fee. Followed by all the drugs, alcohol, and women your mind can dream of.

So, yes, my business thrives, and I am filthy fucking rich, but apart from that, I own a lot of other businesses. My casino is my baby though, and the one thing I treasure out of the many others.

A lot of illegal activities happen on those premises, all with my knowledge, including underground drug runners. Whorehouses around town would love to take me down and take back their parts, which I now own and run more successfully.

You sell drugs on the street?

Well, I will sell them with a shot of the most expensive whiskey, followed by a stripper for your entertainment. And if you have more money to waste, then head into one of our playrooms where you can waste even more money at our tables.

Men love to play, fuck, drink, and get high.

So, yes, I own one of the fastest-growing developments in the country.

Watching my back is how I got this far. I don't trust anyone, because those closest to you are the assholes who usually fuck you over.

That's how my father got caught.

"Someone will knock you off that high horse one day, Atlas."

"Next time, send me a blonde. I'm liking the taste of them lately." I raise my eyebrow to Harry and walk away.

Nodding to Garry to get Theadora, I walk out,

stopping only to look back briefly. I find her laughing at something Benji has said.

That *cannot* happen.

I will put a bullet between her eyes before I let that happen.

CHAPTER NINE

Theadora

Benji is funny and charming, and I can't help but laugh at him. Even when I know I shouldn't. I've kept to *his* rule and haven't spoken all evening. But it's hard not to laugh, and he never told me I couldn't do that.

"Miss..." Atlas's driver walks over to me, "... it's time we leave now."

I look back to Benji. Smiling, I go to walk away when he stops me, his hand softly grabbing my wrist, making me look back to him.

"What's your name? At least tell me that?"

I look to the driver, then back to Benji.

"Theadora." I smile before I follow the driver outside to a waiting car, hoping he won't say anything to Atlas.

Opening the car door, I climb in. I should have looked, but I didn't think Atlas would be in here, not after…

"I told you to *not* make conversation." Atlas eyes me with a skeptical glare.

My eyes narrow at his words as the car starts. "I didn't."

Amber eyes lock on me like magnets. "Did you just lie to me? I thought we had an understanding, Theadora."

I cross my legs and move uneasily in my seat. "No, I didn't! I did as you asked. I did not make *conversation* with anyone. I told one man my name, and that was it."

When I glance up to look at him, he's watching me with stormy eyes.

I look away first. I can't hold that glare too long —it makes me uneasy.

"You told a man you don't know your name? After I told you not to?"

"I know his name," I reply, staring out the window, but not really watching anything.

"Yes, Benji mentioned you." My head flicks around fast at the mention of his name. "You think

I didn't know?" He shakes his head. "You'll come to realize I know almost everything that goes on. Not much gets past me."

"If you know so much, then why do you need me to listen to other people's fucking conversations?" I ask him, crossing my arms over my chest. "And how much longer am I expected to do this shit for?"

Atlas leans forward and knocks on the window between us and the driver slows down to a stop.

"Get out," he says with insatiable anger, and when I look down, his hands are scrunched in fists at his sides.

I look out the window—we're on a highway with cars flying by at top speed.

"What?"

"Get out, Theadora. You think anyone can talk to me the way you just did? No. I usually do worse, like put a bullet in their brain. Now… Get. The. Fuck. Out."

I hear a click of door locks and see the driver get out, and then open my door.

I look back at Atlas. "Fuck you, you stupid prick. You are not a god! You're just a man with way too much power." I go to climb out, but his voice halts me.

"Do you want me to kill Lucy and just end all

of this? Would that be easier than dealing with me?"

Cold wind hits my bare legs as I freeze on the spot.

He can't be serious? Can he?

"No." My eyes blink, but I will never allow tears to fall. I would not give him that pleasure. "No," I whisper, but know he hears me.

"Good! Shut the door and start walking."

I step back and shut the door. My legs shake as I watch his car drive off and start my trek home, but first I remove my sky-high heels.

It took a few miles of walking until I got to the first turn off. Once I made it that far, I ordered an Uber, which I am getting out of right now.

Atlas is standing at his car in front of my house with his legs crossed over at the ankle as he watches me slide out. When I close the door, I walk toward him, but he doesn't move, just stares at me with his brazen eyes.

"I'm too damn tired and cold to deal with you." I shake my head and walk up the few steps to my door.

"What if I offered you a deal you couldn't refuse?" he asks.

It makes me stop. As I slowly turn around to face him, my heart starts beating widely out of my chest.

Watching him push off from the car, he swipes at his bottom lip with his thumb, then looks at me through a flick of hair that seems to have fallen lose from its perfect coiffure.

"What offer?"

He steps forward, knowing he has me. "Do you love her? Is that why you wish to save her?" Atlas asks, his head dropping slightly to the side.

"Yes, she is my sister. Of course I love her."

He nods his head. "But do you like her?"

"What kind of question is that?" I remark while shaking my head.

"Answer the question, Theadora. You can love someone and not like them. Do you like her?"

"How would you know?"

I'm surprised when he answers me. "I love my father, but I do *not* like him." His eyes blaze into mine, and I can almost see the flickering of flames in them. "So, do you like her?" he asks again.

"No," I utter the word but don't break eye contact. "But I am all she has. And I would hope someone would do the same for me if I were in the same situation."

"You think Lucy would save you?" he asks as if he has trouble saying the words.

"No. No, I do not." I let the realization of that sink in, and I start to shake. I'm cold and just want to be in bed, forget about all of this, if only for a few hours.

"Goodnight, Theadora."

"Do you like to control and scare people into what you want them to be?" I ask while opening my front door. Stepping inside, ready to shut the door, I notice he's watching me intently.

"Yes, and it works." Atlas gets into his car, leaving me standing there wondering what type of man I am in business with.

And how the fuck do I get out of this mess I am in.

"Thea! Thea!" My name is yelled, but I bury myself in my bed even farther. "Thea, get your ass up out of bed, we're meant to be running today, and you make me do this shit all the time, even when I want to flake out on you. So get up." Something lands on my head, and I pull the covers back.

"Tina, really?" I pull the covers back over my head.

"Aren't you happy you gave me a key?" She laughs, and then pulls all the blankets from my bed, leaving me with only a pillow. "You do this to me, so now it's payback, baby. Which I might add, I thought the day would never come." Tina laughs, jumping on my bed. "Sleeping in? Who are you, and what have you done with my best friend?"

"I had a big night. I just want to sleep."

"If you don't run, you'll have a bad day, we all know this." I ignore her words, closing my eyes. "When was the last time you ran, Thea?"

"Fucking fine! I'm getting up." I throw the pillow and slide out of bed to get changed.

Tina watches me, waiting for me to answer her question, so she repeats it, "Thea, when was the last time you ran?"

"Last week."

Her mouth goes wide. "A week?" She shakes her head. "You never go that long. What's wrong?"

"Ready?" I ask, putting on my sneakers and tying my hair back.

"You're avoiding my question. It's Lucy, isn't it?"

"Tina, let's just run."

She nods and doesn't push me further; I know

she will once we're done, though. When we step outside, I see a familiar black car pulling up at the front of my house. I start running, and Tina isn't that far behind me. For someone who complains that I make her run with me, she's pretty good at it.

We don't talk. We usually don't, but I can feel her stare penetrating me the whole way there and back. By the time we arrive back at the house, the car is still there and so is *he*.

Why is he here?

Tina comes to a stop next to me and clutches my hand in hers. "Who is that man?" Her voice is raised a little louder than a whisper.

I can't blame her for wanting to know.

Atlas isn't dressed as he was last night, he's dressed in ripped jeans and a white shirt showcasing a lot of his ink, and not just a flower up his arm, no his arms are covered in black ink. I thought he had some tattoos from the ones I saw peeking up his neck, but I did not expect this many.

Risking a glance, I see his eyes lock onto mine.

Tina nudges me again as we walk closer. I totally think about ignoring him. The last thing I need is for him to be a fixture in my life, and my co-workers and friends knowing about him. But I know Tina will not let this go either.

"Tina, this is Atlas."

I watch as she steps forward, her chest rising and falling as she walks toward him offering him her hand. He looks to it, then looks at me. I raise an eyebrow, waiting to see what he will do. He's the one who's showed up at my place on a Sunday morning with no warning after leaving me to fend for myself last night.

"Tina." He takes her hand, leans down, letting his lips brush against her knuckles before he stands and offers her a small smile.

"Oh my God, if you don't marry him, Thea, I will." Tina turns, walks over to me, kisses my cheek, and whispers, "I hope you're hitting that. Hard."

I can't help but giggle at her words before she waves and disappears to her car.

I focus back on Atlas who is now leaning against his car again with his arms crossed over his chest and his lips puckered.

I wonder what he's thinking. What is flying around in that head of his that makes him keep coming back? It can't just be what my sister owes him. If he thought I was going to run, I would have done so already. And I like to run.

"You haven't been running this week."

I wipe a stray piece of hair from my face as he watches me. "I've been busy. You've kept me busy."

"That I have," he agrees.

"Now, if you would kindly tell me why you are here, that would be great."

Atlas pushes off the car and steps to me, looks up at my door, and then back to me. "You should run more," he says, as if he knows everything, then he turns back to his car.

"What do you need me to do?" I ask.

"Relax. I won't need you until next weekend, Theadora."

Scrunching my eyebrows, I shake my head. "So why did you come?"

Opening the car door, he looks me up and down. "Have a good day, Theadora."

"Fuck you, Atlas," I say with a smirk. And those words make his lips twitch.

He nods, then gets into his car and drives off.

I stand on the side of the road watching his car head off in the distance, wondering what on earth he wanted. For what reason did he come here?

Atlas is a mystery, and one I'm not sure I want to figure out.

CHAPTER TEN

Theadora

Flowers still come every day when I'm at work. All from 'A.'

I don't see him that weekend, and when the next weekend comes and goes, I am beginning to get angsty. He was a no show again, and I don't understand how he went from so many times in one week to no contact at all in two weeks.

The following Friday rolls around three weeks after I last saw him, and when I get home that afternoon, he's leaning against his car, looking at his diamond watch when I walk up to him.

"You're late."

"Didn't know I was meeting you," I answer.

He looks up at me from his watch, and his eyes scan me.

"How is my sister?"

"She's fine. Mouthy as usual."

I go to smile at his response, then quickly shake my head and remember we are *not* friends. This man had me kidnapped and is using me to his own advantage.

"Will I get to see her again soon?"

His eyes narrow. "I have work for you tonight. You'll be my date." Turning, Atlas reaches into the car and walks over to hand me a dress.

"I already have two good dresses. I don't need another."

"Take the dress, it's cocktail."

"Am I allowed to speak tonight?"

He holds out the dress, and I take it from his hands. Atlas shoves his hands in his pockets and looks at me. "When asked to." He turns, walks to his car and looks back at me.

"I know. Be ready by six. Right?" I turn, not waiting for his answer as I walk up the stairs to my door. When I turn back around, he's gone, and in my hand is another expensive dress.

After stepping inside, I take my time opening this one. I have a few hours to kill before he'll be back to collect me, to take me to God only knows where.

Atlas is slowly removing my power, and I don't like it.

Pulling out the designer Chanel dress, I almost weep at the sight of it. It has an all-black skirt. The top is made in a flesh-colored mesh with black velvet flowers covering the right parts to give it the look of a top when, in reality, it's basically skin with strategically placed decorations.

It's beautiful.

And my absolute favorite so far.

Getting dressed is easy, and it fits like it was made for my body. My nipples are covered by the black velvet flowers, and a few are scattered over my belly, with a few on the back too. But mostly, I am bare from the waist up. A dress like this deserves a great hairstyle, so I have put my hair up with loose curls and a black flower to the side. I paired the ensemble with black heels.

Once I am completely dressed, I pour myself a wine, because if previous events are anything to go by, I will not be drinking. And I really need a damn drink. Wine in hand, a knock comes on the door, so I drink it fast until it's empty, before I open it, knowing it is going to be Atlas.

As soon as I see him dressed again in a black

suit, I have to remember to not stare. Atlas's eyes flick to my wine glass, then back to my face, assessing me.

"How many?"

"One," I say, telling him the truth.

He nods, then walks to his car. I place my wine glass down on the nearby table and follow him out, making sure I have my purse and keys.

Atlas holds the car door open for me. I slide in, and he watches the way my body moves. I can feel his eyes glued to me. Fuck! I was glued to my body too when I looked in the mirror. This dress would make a six look like a ten, that's the kind of magic it holds.

"Do you plan to give me instructions for tonight?" I ask when he gets in.

The car takes off, and I turn to look at him. His head is down, looking at his cell phone.

"The plans I had for you aren't really working out. So change of plans," he says, not looking up.

"What were the plans?" I ask.

Turning to look at me, he says, "You were to do a lot of things you more than likely wouldn't be comfortable with."

"You play me like a chess piece, and now you're pulling me off the board and calling what? Checkmate? I'm confused." I shake my head. "What was it you would have had me doing?" The car comes to a stop, and he turns to get out. "Tell me, Atlas. What would you have had me do?"

He turns to look at me, leans over and grabs hold of my face, gripping it hard between his fingers. "I would have used and abused you in ways you can only imagine."

"How?" I manage to speak, though I am shocked by his words.

"You would have been a pawn. I would have made you suck the cock of my enemy to get what I wanted, just like that girl did to me. I would throw you to the wolves and wouldn't care what they did to you, as long as you came out with valuable information, if that's what was needed." His breath is heavy on my face with his closeness. Atlas squeezes my face just a second longer before he drops his hands and pulls back. "Now stop questioning me before I decide to make you pay your sister's debt back by getting on your knees for me." He leaves the car as I sit there, more than a little shocked. My cheeks now hurting from his firm grip, and wondering if I should have thrown meat at the tiger like that and not have expected him to bite me back. Because if I am not careful, soon he may just feed me to the wolves.

My door opens, and the driver stands there with

Atlas in front of him, his elbow extended, waiting for me. Blowing out a breath, I slide out and take his waiting arm. He doesn't even glance at me before he starts walking.

We enter a ballroom, and the minute we do, I know we are rubbing elbows with the elite. I spot a public figure straight away. He offers a small head nod to Atlas who gives one back in return.

"Mr. Hyde, so good to see you in attendance tonight."

I almost let the shock of his last name show on my face. Almost.

Hyde? Really? Gosh, that suits him more than he will ever know.

Atlas glances at me as if he knows my reaction and pins me with a stare before he looks back at the man who's talking to him. I pay no attention. Politics has never interested me, just like gambling never did.

"Yes, good…" is all he says in return.

I guess it's not just me he doesn't give much conversation to.

"And who is this fine lady?" His hand is offered, and I go to place mine in it, but Mr. Hyde, aka Atlas, pulls me back.

"This… is no one of interest to you."

"Oh, no sharing?" he jokes, but I look at Atlas, and somehow, I don't think it's a joke.

Atlas starts walking and pulls me along with him to the next group of people. He says his hellos to about a million people—okay, slight exaggeration—until we finally greet two more people before we get to sit. When we do finally take a seat, my feet are thankful, as these heels are killing me.

"You don't talk or seem to like most of these people. So why are you here?" I ask as we sit mostly in silence.

A waiter walks past, and I eye the glasses of champagne, but I know better than to drink while he's around. When I get back home after this shitshow I will get drunk. I need it. And I'm not even much of a drinker normally.

"Did I ask for conversation?" he snaps.

A hand is placed on his shoulder, and he turns his hard eyes to the source of it. A woman, more than likely around my age, smiles down at him but quickly removes her hand.

"Mr. Hyde was hoping to have a word, sir." She looks down at me, then back to him. "Privately."

Atlas stands, straightens his suit jacket, and walks away. He doesn't need to tell me not to move because I do not see that happening at all. My feet are aching, and we had been walking and standing in the same spot for about two hours. This has become very boring, and I don't even know why I am here.

The chair next to me scrapes as I pick up a piece of finger food from the middle of the table. Turning, I see the man from earlier when we first walked in, take the seat. His hungry eyes eat up my dress, and all of a sudden, the dress I was in love with makes me feel naked and exposed in a way I didn't think I would feel.

"Didn't think he would leave you alone." He smiles, placing a glass of champagne in front of me. I don't touch it nor thank him for it. "Seems he has an interest in you. Atlas always shares his women. So, what I want to know…" he leans closer so his breath hits the side of my neck, "… what's so special about you?"

I know this man. He's a politician and married with kids. Yet, here he is asking me why Atlas can't share me.

And that thought makes me sick.

"What's your name?" he asks, to which I ignore him. It's not him I came with, and it's not him I am scared of. No. The man I came with, and am equally scared of, is also a man I am attracted to. And that little indiscretion is an issue within itself.

"It's not wise to ignore someone when they speak to you."

I scoff and turn around to see if Atlas is coming back. A hard hand lands on my leg, and I still. Turning around, I notice the dirty politician has a gleam in his eyes as he stares at me.

"You're just a whore. Whores speak as they are told. So when I speak to you, you answer. Right, whore?"

I lean in close, my hand moving to his leg, then I sneak it up, catch hold of his dick, and squeeze. "Get your filthy fucking hands off me before I squash your cock so hard, I will break it. And don't ever speak to a woman like that again, you pig." I squeeze his cock even harder for good measure as his hand breaks free from my leg. The minute I free his cock, he stands, towering over me.

"Is there a problem here?" I never thought I would be soothed by that voice, but I am.

Dirty politician asshole looks to Atlas, then back at me. "Keep your whores in line." He purses his lips in anger before he turns and walks away.

Letting go of a breath I didn't know I was holding, I finally relax.

"Get up, we're leaving." I turn at that voice, that extremely angry voice, and with it, stormy eyes are directed at me.

Shit! Shit!

Standing, he doesn't offer me his hand, and I watch as he wipes at his lips.

Is that red lipstick stained on them?

Fuck! What do I care?

As soon as we push out the door, we walk down the street to where I see his car waiting. The minute we reach it, he opens the door and instructs me to get in, which I do, and he follows. Atlas is quiet for the entire drive home.

Once we finally reach my house, which is outside of the city, I am more than thankful to get out and away from him, except he follows me to my door. I unlock it and turn to him, but before I can say a word, I'm being pushed inside, his hand going to my waist as he shoves me to the nearest wall, my back hitting it hard.

"Who the fuck do you think you are?" His stormy amber eyes search mine.

CHAPTER ELEVEN

Atlas

I have been gentle when there has been no need for it. I have been patient, and I don't even fucking know why. It's not like she deserves it, and if she was any other woman, I would not be gentle nor patient. She would do as I ask with no questions.

But not her, not Theadora.

My hands grip her tiny waist as I hold her to the wall, her blue eyes, which shine so fucking bright, bore into me.

Have you ever looked at the sky and thought, what a fucking beautiful blue?

Well, that's her eyes.

Not an ocean blue, like I first thought.

"Wh… what," she stutters, her back against the wall, my hands unable to move from her hips.

"Who do you think you are?" I ask again, my hips moving forward close enough to touch her.

"I don't understand."

My head shakes. "That man you just threatened is a customer, and a good one. You were seen with me. So, he knows you are one of mine." Her eyes go wide at my words. "Maybe I should make it up to him and give you to him as a gift." Now my body touches hers, and despite her being shocked and angry, her cheeks flush.

Her hands lift and push against my chest, and I take a step back. "That shit wasn't a part of our deal. I am not a whore."

My free hand reaches up and strokes her face while she sucks in a deep breath.

"But you would be a perfect whore."

Her eyes go wide at my words, and I see a little break there, the way the brightness that was shining seems lost now.

"How much longer am I expected to do this?"

I turn to look at her. "Until the debt is paid."

"I'll get a loan and pay back what's left. How much?"

"You accepted the agreement. You will continue to work it off as I see fit. Until then, don't question me."

Her eyes thin and her lips scrunch. "You are a real asshole. You know that, right?"

She isn't telling me anything new. I don't plan on being her friend, but she's pushing every damn available button I have. Never have I let a woman speak to me, or disrespect those I am in business with, the way she does.

"Nothing to say? That means you know it." Her head drops as she tries to give me her best 'fuck you' face. "Give. Me. My. Sister. You are making me your bitch, the least you can do is give me Lucy back."

I smirk, that's not happening.

"So, that gets a reaction from you." She clenches her hands. I think she is about to walk off and shut the door when she turns back around to face me. "Stop sending me dresses, it's inappropriate." Theadora turns her nose up at me as I take a step back.

"If I knew you wouldn't come to an event dressed like a slob like every other time I have seen you out of this house, I would stop. But I have an appearance to keep up, and you don't meet those standards without appropriate attire.".

Her mouth drops open, she slams the door shut in my face, and I smile before I turn to leave.

"And how is the lady in pink going?" Benji asks. He sits down at my desk, kicks his feet up as if he owns the fucking place.

"Fine."

"Please, tell me more. Have you fucked her yet, or even tried?"

I look up at him and eye his feet, he removes them with a chuckle.

"I'll take that as a no. I feel she may be an exception to your possibilities. I mean, you get pussy just by looking at chicks, but this one… she is different, that's for sure."

"I don't give a fuck how different she is, as long as she serves her purpose."

"And what purpose is that? Because from what I can see, you are getting her to do sweet fuck all. You don't need spies, let's be real, Atlas. Only someone very stupid would betray you."

I eye him. "Why are you here?"

He stands, walks to the window that overlooks the inside of the casino, and stays where he is.

"You want something?" I ask, my fingers dragging across the desk. "What do you want?"

"Give her to me," he says, turning back to me. "Give me her, please?"

"No. I told you before."

He shakes his head, his blond hair no longer perfect as he strokes his fingers through it.

"I need her. Just give her to me, Atlas."

"Go home, Benji."

He slams his fists into my wall, making a hole in the plasterboard, then he straightens his posture. "I'll get her. You can't be a god all the time, Atlas."

I smile. "Who says I can't?"

Benji backs away and doesn't say another word as he leaves the room. When he does, Garry walks in, looking back at Benji before he shuts the door.

"Do you want her to do it? Are you sure?"

"No. No, I am not." I move to the same wall Benji was at and inspect the damage. "But this way her debt will be paid faster, and she can be out of my life."

Garry departs, leaving me standing there wondering about possibilities that can never happen.

CHAPTER TWELVE

Theadora

As Chloe and her husband walk in, I watch closely. Chloe comes straight to my office as her husband walks around talking to all the women. Why she is with him I will never know.

Chloe offers me a smile before she takes the seat in front of me, one leg crossing over the other. "You wouldn't believe the week I've had."

I smile. She is my boss, so I take the time, even if I don't have any for small talk. I am, after all, trying to run her business, which she is hardly a part of. She leaves everything to me.

"I bet it was crazy," I reply because it usually is. How they have a successful business still baffles me. When I first started, I was her first employee, and we built this business up. Well, I did with her funds and encouragement, and now we are one of the biggest online sellers in the country. I never left because I don't know much else, and more importantly, to walk away would break my heart. This job helped me support Lucy when our parents died.

"It was, but look… I need you to fire at least five employees."

My mouth goes wide, and my eyebrows draw together.

What on earth?

"Umm…" I stand, walking to my door and shutting it before I turn back around to face her. This doesn't make any sense. I see the money rolling in. I know she earns in the millions, and it is more than enough to cover her employees, and on top of that we need our employees. I don't hire out of the fun of it; each girl in this office has a job to do, and by getting rid of even one it will make my workload even larger than it already is. Unfortunately, there aren't two of me, so I need to know what's going on.

"Look, I know. You don't see it, but I need it

done. Don't question me, Thea, just do it." She stands, throwing her bag over her shoulder.

I cross my arms over my chest. "Any preferences on who? Because I need every one of the girls in this office."

Chloe gives me an eye roll as her husband walks over and opens the door, he leans in and kisses my cheek, making me want to spew instantly. I get creepy vibes from him and have never liked him. But in all the years I've been here, he hasn't made a move apart from kissing my cheek, thank God.

"Jesse, good to see you."

I put on a fake smile. He doesn't work. As far as I know, he does nothing but spend Chloe's money.

"Yes, well, sorry it can't be under better circumstances," he offers with a shake of his head.

Fake.

I was not born yesterday.

"I'm sure Chloe has told you, you're to let some staff go."

"Yes, yes, she did." I look to Chloe who's busy staring at her perfectly varnished nails. "She was just going to tell me why. Unless you want to?"

"Oh, you know I don't handle the business side of things, that's all her. I just support her and what she needs to do."

And spend, he forgot to add.

"Chloe?" I ask, looking at her. I once thought she was the coolest person ever, to put so much trust in me and support me as I threw ideas her way that she let me run with. Now? Well, now, I am not so sure.

Chloe looks up from her nails and offers me an eye roll. "You are replaceable, too, Thea. Just remember that," she spits at me.

When did she become so volatile?

"Yes, which you have just made perfectly clear. I simply have to have a reason for your employees when I fire them, is all."

She flicks her hand at me. "I'm sure you will think of something, Thea. You always do."

A hand touches my shoulder. "You are a gem, Thea. What would we do without you?"

Die.

That's what I scream at him in my head, but then I remember I'm a nice girl, and nice girls don't talk shit to their bosses.

"I guess we will never know." I smile.

"I'll be in tomorrow to make sure you do it."

"You can, you know. If it's urgent. Fire them, I mean?"

Chloe looks out my office to all the girls on the floor. There are at least thirty of them, each one doing their own part to make the business run successfully. From marketing, packing, checking orders, and returns, to the concierge part of the online business. Who to fire will not be an easy decision, and it's not something I want to do, considering I personally hired each of these girls. Each one chosen for their strengths and work ethics. Not once have I had to let someone go, because when I hire them I do it right. Not haphazardly, like Chloe did when we first started. Because she had no idea and couldn't have given the first fuck about any of them. She paid me half the wage I should have been earning at the time, which I never complained about, even though it's illegal. And when she made her first million—thanks to me—I asked for a pay rise, which she actually agreed to. I'm sure I could take my skills and go get what I'm rightfully meant to be paid. But that would mean leaving something I've built, something that gives me joy. And that scares the hell out of me.

"You no longer want to do your job?" Jesse asks.

I turn to look at him. His hair, which has way too much product in it, and his high-end shirt, which is mustard in color, mixed with gray slacks… honestly, he looks like a dick. A man with money who's supported by his wife.

My cell starts ringing, allowing me to dodge answering his question, and we all turn to look at it.

"You take personal calls while at work now?" Chloe asks.

"Considering I work more than the required hours, I need to have my phone on me in case of an emergency," I answer with a smile.

She doesn't reply, she knows I work more than I should, and even weekends, which she doesn't pay me for, when we have a big drop or sale. Yet, I don't complain, because when it's just the girls and me, I do love my job.

"Nice flowers," Jesse says, walking over and touching them.

"You can have them." I smile, walking around my desk.

"I will fire two girls at your request. I can simply not let go more than that, or else I will need a pay raise for the number of extra hours I will need to work to cover their department, and up to the correct amount I'm owed."

Both of them stand still and stare at me.

Chloe then looks over at her husband, and he nods. Then he offers me his goodbye as he walks out, leaving Chloe and me in the office alone.

"Will you tell me the real reason I have to let go of my girls?"

Chloe looks down to the floor with a slightly

guilty expression. "I have to do what's best for him… and this is what's best for him right now."

"Okay." I know that's all she will give me. She loves that idiot of a man, and he uses her for all she's worth. We all know he sleeps around on her, and she just doesn't seem to care. It's quite sad really.

"You aren't replaceable, Thea. I do value you. It's just been a lot lately."

I nod. I know I'm not replaceable. If there was no me, I don't know what would happen to this place. When I take holidays, which is exceedingly rare, it has to be when things are slow, and Marissa usually helps me out.

"I'll do it, okay? I may not be happy about it, but I will do it."

Chloe nods, then walks to the door and looks back.

"When should I expect to see you again?" I ask.

She shrugs. "When another cut is needed."

Goddamn! I cringe at her words as she walks out.

Fuck.

I fired two girls the next day, as I was told, and I

despised it. I dislike Chloe for making me do it. They did nothing wrong, and they all show up and do their work without problems.

Arriving home that weekend after the week I had, I pour myself a wine, and when a knock on the door comes, I ignore it. I know it's going to be him wanting me to do some stupid bullshit task to help pay back my sister's money.

But I don't want to.

I am sick of it.

Sick of everything right now.

Putting the full bottle to my lips, I drink down more—way more than I should.

The knocking stops, and when it does, I get up and find myself another bottle of wine and start on that one too. That's when the knocking comes again. Walking over to the door, I pull it open to find Atlas standing there. I blink a few times to make sure as my vision is hazy.

He is a hard man to not see. I mean, with all those hard edges, I bet my tongue could lick them all and keep exploring.

"Edges?" Atlas asks.

Fuck! I shake my head as I lock my eyes on him. Did I just say that out loud?

"Do you have two nose rings, or am I seeing double?" I ask.

He looks down to the wine in my hand and steps forward, taking it from me. "How much of this have you had?" he asks as if he has some sort of right to know.

"It for sure looks like two bottles." I go to touch his nose rings, ignoring him, and he swats my hand away. "Theadora."

"One…" I point without touching, "… two." I nod my head. "Okay, you have two. Why don't you wear both all the time? They look good," I tell him with a smile.

Atlas rolls up his sleeves, and I see his tattooed arms.

"Holy shit! Now that's some ink. Where else is it?" I ask, stepping forward, ready to lift his shirt when he blocks me. Atlas steps into my house and walks straight past me. He heads to my kitchen, and I follow him as he enters like he owns it. My eyes drop to his gorgeous ass, and I am way too busy staring while he's poured me a drink of water and hands it to me.

"Get dressed. But first, drink this."

I look down at the old shirt I am wearing—which is just that, a shirt—and smile as I reach for the water. Taking a large sip, I drink it all, handing him back the empty glass.

"Get dressed, Theadora," he instructs.

I walk past him to my bedroom and quickly find a dress—that isn't worth a few thousand dollars—and slip it over my shoulders so it falls down my thighs before I reach for my cell and walk back out.

"Dressed," I say with a smile, then a twirl. My shoes are in my hand, and he reaches for them, taking them and bending down to put them on my feet. His hand touches my ankle, and an intake of breath happens so fast at his electric touch, I'm close to asking him to move those hands, but instead he does one shoe up carefully. When he's strapped the first, his hand slides just a fraction, quickly releasing, before he goes to the next and repeats. When he looks up at me, I shut my gaping mouth. He just shakes his head and walks out the door. "In the car."

I roll my eyes at his bossy words but follow, getting in beside him. The car takes off, and I sit back and close my eyes, trying to sober up and remove the thoughts of his touch, which are still scorching my skin.

"You drank way too much." His voice is between a whisper and a shout but not gentle enough to be normal.

"Yes, Father."

"If you were my child you would be over my knee."

My heart rate picks up at his tone of voice. "That can be arranged." I forgot to mention I'm a whore when drunk. And let's face it, Atlas is the prettiest man I've ever seen.

"Did you just…" He shakes his head and looks out the window. "You sound like your sister right now," he says with a wave of disappointment. Well, at least I think that's what it is, from what I can tell.

"Same mother, different fathers, will do that to you," I tell him truthfully.

"How did you turn out like this, and she like…" He doesn't finish that sentence, but it still makes me angry.

I shrug. "Lucy feels everything and wants everything. She has a self-entitlement about her." My head starts to spin as the car comes to a stop at a warehouse. I can feel his eyes on me, but I choose not to look his way as I open the door, needing fresh air urgently. Stepping out, my heel slips on something wet and sticky. So I look down, and when the blur fades, I follow the dark puddle. It belongs to the politician who touched my leg and called me a whore. The wet substance on the floor is his blood.

A scream rips through me as I stumble back, trying to escape.

CHAPTER THIRTEEN

Theadora

I feel like I should give a tutorial on how to get sober really quickly.

Finding a dead body would be at the top of the list, that's for sure.

In my escape to step back, Atlas grabs me before I can move any farther, and breathes in my ear. That minty breath I smelled all those weeks ago, a reminder now of what an evil man Atlas really is.

"What..." I shake my head, not knowing what to say, but he doesn't let me go. Atlas keeps me standing where I am, in my heels, in a pool of blood, with his hands holding me in place.

If he let go, I would fall to the floor.

"He was looking for you. Wanted you. Started asking around about you," he whispers, moving a stray piece of hair from my ear and tucking it behind so he can lick my earlobe. "When something is mine, no one can have it, want it, or even think about hurting it."

The way he says it makes me want to run.

Am I that to him—an *it*.

"I am not yours," I tell him.

Atlas bites my earlobe, dragging his teeth over it until it pops out, and he smells me again. "For now, you are. You just haven't realized it yet."

"People will ask about him, he will be missed," I say while shaking my head.

"They will, but no one will link it back to me." He steps away, setting me free, and I take a long, slow breath. My white heels are now red. Every step I take makes the blood move, and I have droplets of the man's blood on my toes. "But you…" he says, making me freeze. "He was asking about you. Who is this woman that embarrassed him in a public forum? Who is she?" he says, smirking. And it's evil that smirk.

And I am instantly sober.

"Why would you do that?" I ask, looking back to the politician lying on the cement floor, his eyes wide open in death. I look over my shoulder and see the red door—it's the same place he had me brought to the night I was kidnapped. "You had planned to kill me," I say with realization.

"I did," he replies without hesitation.

"Why didn't you?"

"I found a use for you after all."

"Is what Lucy did really that bad?" I ask. "It's only money which you seem to have a lot of."

"Yes, yes, I do. And yes, what she did was. So, in comes you to the rescue." He brushes a stray hair from my face tenderly as his voice is whispered with nothing but sweet venom.

Why does he hate me so much?

What have I ever done to him that would have affected him like this?

Not a damn thing!

"Will I end up the same way as him?" I flick my hand to the man on the floor.

Did he do it with his own two hands?

Or did he have someone else to do it?

What kind of man is Atlas? Really?

And why haven't I tried to find out more about him? That's another question shooting through my foggy brain right at this moment.

Two men walk out, both are dressed in hazmat suits. They step over to the body, pick it up, then carry it out while I stand frozen, unable to move as I look down at the blood that still coats the floor.

"Who are you?" I ask with a shaky breath, my eyes fixated on the blood, but my question directed to Atlas. I hear his boots click on the floor as he walks over to me, lifting my chin with one finger as he smiles at me. His other hand touches my cheek, stroking it, making goosebumps break free all over me.

"Now you're asking the right questions." His voice is intoxicating and scary all in one hit. I hiccup, and when I do, I spew all over his shirt. He drops my chin and steps back. Touching the edges of his shirt, he pulls it over his head and lets it drop to the floor. I wipe my mouth as I look up at him and shake my head.

"Put it back on," I say while wiping my mouth, he hands me a bottle of water and I rinse my mouth. It's unfair to have to look at someone as gorgeous as him and dislike him so much all at the same time.

His chest looks like a puzzle piece with a flower on his collarbone and women up and down his arms. There's a gun on his left, with a devil on his right arm.

Who the fuck is this man?

His whole chest and arms are covered, and not one of the tattoos is cheery. They are all dark, and each one represents something I more than likely do not want to know about.

"No," he says, referring to what I just said.

His chest is hard, I can tell just by looking at it, and his arms are all muscle. If he lifted me and pressed me against him, I bet I would feel all his hard edges.

No, can't have those thoughts.

I blame the alcohol.

"How do I leave? Get me out of this place. Why did you even bring me here?" I scream the last part at him. My hands lift in fists as I step closer to him, not even caring about the blood beneath my shoes anymore. "Why did you bring me here?"

His lips, soft and hard, come down on me. In one swift and fast movement, he claims me as his without my permission. His arm circles my waist, pulling my body flush with his while the other cradles my head, keeping my lips to his.

I go to push away my hands banging on his chest, but he bites my lip until I open my mouth, then he tastes me. I freeze, liking the way he has me, and the way he feels against my lips, so I close my eyes.

Just for a second.

A second is all it takes for me to think this man isn't bad and he wants me for normal reasons, not reasons that involve blackmail or using me.

But I'm wrong, so I bite his lip until I taste blood, expecting him to pull away, but he doesn't. He simply cackles between my lips and presses his harder to mine, all the while pulling my body even closer.

Feeling him against me doesn't help my resolve in wanting him to go away. No, it does anything but, and soon I'm pushing myself against him as my body starts to crave him and has a mind of its own, moving to get as much friction as possible.

My breathing becomes harder, and my chest rises and falls at the same time my hips do, my head spins, and I'm lost, until someone coughs, and it breaks the haze he has me under. Pulling away, he lets me until I back up and end up slipping, my hands landing in blood and a dress I once loved is now covered in it.

Looking up at him, I more than likely look like that girl in the movie *Carrie*, but I don't care, as long as I am not losing my own sense of worth and rubbing myself all over him like a two-bit hooker.

"Clean yourself up," he says as someone passes him a shirt, which he easily throws on.

I look down at my stained shoes and dress and know every item will have to be burned. So when I stand, I start to remove them. Stepping out of the blood, I begin with my shoes first, one at a time undoing the straps he did up so delicately, and dropping them until they are both off, followed by my dress. Now, I am standing in front of him in nothing but panties and a lame excuse for a bra.

His eyes devour me, lust apparent in their depths. It's the first real emotion I have seen from him apart from his evil laughter. When he catches me staring at him, he shuts his facial expressions down and walks over to one of his guys and clicks his fingers. The guy removes his shirt and hands it over, which Atlas then hands to me.

"Put this on and leave your shit including your panties, they have blood on them. It will all be burned."

I have no reason to trust him.

For all I know he could use my clothes as evidence, and say it was me who put a bullet in the politician's brain. After all, I am covered in the man's blood. But I'm too tired to argue, and I do as he says and get in his car, leaving my favorite dress and shoes behind at a crime scene.

The car ride is uncomfortable, there's no other word to describe it. Stopping out the front of my house, I go to get out when his hand touches my thigh, halting me. Turning back to look at him, his eyes are cast down on my thigh before they slowly creep back up to mine.

"Shower all that off of you." He gestures to the blood, and I can only manage to stare at him as I get out. "Someone will be back for the shirt. Make sure you wrap it in a plastic bag, don't leave it anywhere it will mark."

Turning to close the door, I look down at him. "Why did you kiss me?" I ask, wanting to know if he will answer me.

At first, I think he's going to shut the door and leave me with no explanation, like he does best, but instead he looks at me. "Because you are kissable." He smirks, then shuts the door.

Kissable? What the ever-loving fuck does that mean.

Walking up the steps, I go to open the door, but before I do, it's pulled open, and Tina is standing there. She stares down at my legs and back up, her eyes go wide as she looks behind me to Atlas who's sitting in the car watching us.

"Don't scream. Don't say a word," I tell her.

She listens and steps back, so I follow her. I turn

around to angry eyes as the heavens above rain down a torrential storm, then I shut the front door.

"I need to shower," I say, locking it behind me.

That damn man probably has a key for all I know. He seems to know and have access to things he shouldn't.

"I'm coming." I don't protest, I'm too tired to do so.

Tina follows me in as I turn on the water, stripping off the shirt and placing it in a bag as requested, then get in.

"Just say it," I call out while washing my hair.

I can feel her staring at me.

"Who is he? And what the fuck are you covered in?" She looks me up and down, and I look at her. "Paint…" She pauses, and I can see her thinking. "Is that… blood?" She shoots her eyebrows up.

"No. He's involved with Lucy. We went to an art studio, and this is the outcome." I tell her an utter lie. It hurts to do so because I don't lie to Tina. Finishing up, I get out, and she hands me a towel. "You would tell me, right. If it was something else?"

"Yes, you know I would." She nods, but I get the feeling she doesn't believe me.

"So, he's with Lucy. I had such high hopes with the way he looks at you."

"How does he look at me?" I question. To me,

he stares as if I'm a nuisance. Which baffles me, because I never asked him to be in my life.

"Like he's hungry," she says, turning and walking into my bedroom.

My hand touches my lips from when he kissed me, and I have to try to remember how he looked at me. *Anger.* Anger is all I seem to remember. How can Tina see that, and all I see is hatred?

"I know you're thinking about it. But it is hunger. That man wants you as much as he doesn't," she calls out to me.

I take a look in the mirror at my bruised lips and shake my head at thoughts of him entering my mind.

He isn't welcome.

And I hope all thoughts of him go away forever.

CHAPTER FOURTEEN

Atlas

Killing her friend is playing on my mind right now. Will Theadora tell her? She had to have noticed she was covered in blood.

Did Theadora tell her?

That bastard deserved to die. And anyone who looks for things that are mine will meet the same fate. This isn't an option, and he knew this, and still he went looking for her. I can't fix stupid, and that's exactly what he was. Stupid.

His body will be found as a suicide, and no trace will come back to me. Luckily for me, the people who he hired to find Theadora work for me. So the first thing they did was tell me.

News articles will read, 'Beloved Politician Commits Suicide.' Let's hope for Theodora's sake the same thing won't be said for her friend.

Theadora runs on Sundays like clockwork, but she hasn't been doing that for quite some time.

I'm waiting out the front of her house where she would normally come out dressed in her sweats because the temperature is dropping, but after thirty minutes tick by and there's no sign of her, I walk up to her door and knock. At first, she doesn't answer, but then I hear her footsteps as I give it another firm knock. She pauses, there are no words or movement beyond the door in front of me.

"I should warn you, I have very low patience," I say, knowing she's on the other side.

"I could be sleeping."

"You aren't, so open the door."

She goes silent, but I don't hear her walking away. "Theadora," I say, my patience growing thinner with each passing second.

Finally, she pulls open the door with a scowl sitting on her pretty pink lips. "What is it you do exactly that gives you so much free time to annoy me?" Her eyes pin me with a glare. "Seriously, what do you do?"

"I dabble in a lot of things, but my first love is my casino. I grew it from backyard gambling, and now I am the richest person in this town thanks to it."

"So, you're a dirty casino owner?" she says with venom.

"It didn't start off that way, but yes. How I make a lot of my money is dirty, and Theadora…" I step up closer to her, "… I will do anything to keep my business safe and operating."

"So, why are you here? Why are you annoying me?"

"What did you tell her?" I ask, and her eyes go wide. She shakes her head slowly from side to side.

"Don't you dare threaten Tina. Don't you dare." Her bottom lip quivers.

"What. Did. You. Tell. Her?"

"That we went painting. She thinks it's paint."

"Good." I believe her. She's proving to be nothing like her sister, Lucy.

It's then she looks me up and down and squints. "Why are you dressed like that?" She's staring at my gray track pants and black shirt. She's dressed in a shirt that comes down to her knees, and she has fuzzy socks covering her feet.

I look back outside, then turn to face her. "You run. I run. We are going to run together. Now."

Her face is shocked as she stares at me. "You want to run with me?" she asks in disbelief.

"Did I stutter and not make sense?"

She bites her lip and looks down. "You don't even like me. Why would you want to run with me?"

"We are going to get to know one another. So that starts with me running with you today." My eyes scan her body. "Now, hurry up and get dressed." I turn and start my stretching routine. When I don't hear her move, I turn around, and she's still standing there staring at me as if I have grown a second head. "Theadora." My voice seems to snap her out of her trance, and she turns, running to her room. She doesn't keep me waiting too long, and soon she's out, dressed in tights and a long-sleeved shirt and joggers. Her hair is up in a messy ponytail with AirPods in her ears.

"I don't talk when I run, so keep up and shut up," she tells me. I smirk at her as she starts to stretch. She bends over in front of me, and it takes everything in me not to reach out and touch her ass. When she stands, she stretches one arm and looks behind her, at me.

"Can you keep up?" she asks.

"The question is… can you?" I take off, and it doesn't take her long to catch up. Theadora runs next to me, never once slowing her pace. She's fast. I knew she liked to run, but I didn't expect her to be this quick. When we get to a crossing, I come to a stop, but she stays jogging on the spot, and before I can say a word, the light changes, and she's off again. I never expected I would have to keep up with her, but somehow, I do. When we reach the end of her trail, she slows down and jogs on the spot while removing one AirPod, and she isn't even out of breath.

"Did you run track?" I ask.

"Yes." She looks at me, waiting for me to keep talking.

I damn well didn't expect to be outrun, but she has great stamina. "Go. I'll catch up."

She eyes me suspiciously and does just that, starts running back in the direction we came.

Theadora is sitting out the front of her house with two bottles of water in her hands when I get back. She passes me one as I sit next to her.

"No one keeps up with me, don't be ashamed." Her voice is playful. But what she doesn't know is that I succeed in almost everything I do. Losing is never an option. "Don't be so sour," she says, nudging me. "You will set your face in a permeant scowl one day."

I turn to look at her and see her smiling. It's genuine. Until she realizes I am not, and I watch as it drops from her pink lips.

"You are good. Why have you stopped?" I ask.

"Why are you here?" she asks, back to avoiding my question.

I think on it a bit. I could tell her the truth, but that would do no one any good. So, instead, I offer her a half-truth. "You are meant to be a means to an end. Instead, I am getting lost somewhere in the middle."

She's quiet, and when I turn to look at her, she's staring up at the sky.

"I'm not Lucy. I don't chase or want to be chased by someone who is bad. Bad and me just don't mix. It doesn't entice me nor make me all hot and bothered. She has always wanted the bad boy, while I am more than content to have a man who tells me every day how much I mean to him, instead of letting me guess." When I don't speak, she turns to look at me. "So, use me the same way you would her, Atlas. Because I don't want this game. I didn't sign up for it. All I want is for this to be over so I can go back to my normal life."

I stand at her words. She looks up at me with

her sky-blue eyes, and I wonder how someone can be so perfect.

"You and Lucy are different, that is no lie," I tell her. "One is better than the other, that's for sure," I say while walking away to the waiting car.

I will let her ponder over my words, wondering which I prefer.

CHAPTER FIFTEEN

Theadora

'One is better than the other, that's for sure.' What on earth does that even mean? I watch as he gets in his car, then he looks back.

"When should I be expecting you again?" I ask while standing, my hands running down my sides smoothing my shirt.

His hands are on the wheel. "We can run tomorrow." Then he's gone, pulling out into traffic so quickly the wheels spin.

Tomorrow? Shit!

I don't want to run with him tomorrow. He is a

distraction enough as it is. And his cryptic words make him hard to understand.

Getting inside, my cell starts ringing. I look at the caller ID and don't recognize it, so I start undressing. When it rings again, I contemplate ignoring it because it would be the smart thing to do. It's what I'd usually do, but something pulls me to it, and soon I'm answering.

"Thea." My name is sung into the phone.

I know that voice, and I know it well.

"Lucy," I say, surprised.

"Yes. Look, Thea, I don't have long. He's on his way back."

"Who, Lucy?"

"Sir…" she pauses. "I mean Atlas. He went out this morning, and I snuck one of the men's cell phones. Listen, Thea, you need to get away. Don't worry about me. Don't worry about Atlas. Just go."

"Lucy… I signed up to help because you stole from him."

"I had to," she screams.

"Lucy…" It's always the same with her. She gets herself worked up into a state where you have to calm her down with a soft voice. "Calm down and breathe."

"He likes you. And Atlas doesn't like anyone," she says between harsh breathes. "Honestly. He doesn't like anyone, Thea, and he likes you. Run. Now." Then she hangs up the phone before she says any more. Looking down at my cell, I want to call the number back, but I can't because she rang from a private number. Grabbing my keys, I head out the front and start running straight to Lucy's home. Reaching the stairs, I take them two at a time, and when I finally get to the front door, it's shut. It's not locked, which I didn't expect it to be, as every other time I have come here it's been open, so I head straight in to Lucy's room and start going through her things. Her drawers consist of a lot of underwear and skimpy clothing. What the hell does she do when it gets cold, freeze?

My cell rings again, and this time I'm too eager to answer it. "Lucy," I say, hoping it will be her again.

"So, she did ring you." Atlas's strong voice comes through, so I do the only thing I can think of, I hang up on him and throw my cell phone. Lifting her mattress, I look underneath. When I do, I stop dead. There are pictures. Pictures of me. Pictures of Atlas. But none are taken of me in a sisterly way. No. These are pictures taken without my consent and without my knowledge.

Lifting one up, I look at it. I'm wearing my red skirt with knee-high brown boots. I remember this day. I had to meet with Chloe as we went brand shopping, and Jesse, her husband, was out of town. Why has she got pictures of us? And why are they under her bed?

Reaching for a picture of Atlas, it's one of him in his familiar black suit getting out of his car with a woman by his side, who I know as the lady who delivers my dresses. She doesn't look happy, but then again, she probably never does.

I collect the pictures and stuff them into a bag. I knock on the other bedroom door, Mandy's room, to let her know I'm here. She's probably too high to even know it's me. Or even care, for that matter.

"Mandy." There's no answer when I call out her name. Knocking again, the door opens a few inches, and I see Mandy lying on her bed with her eyes wide open. I freeze, the bag in my hand dropping to the floor at the same time my cell starts ringing again.

"Hello," I say in shock. How I manage to speak any words surprises me.

"Theadora."

"She's dead! I think she's dead," I say, my voice quivering as I walk closer. I look at her chest and hope and pray she's sleeping with her eyes open, and that her chest is actually moving. Closing my eyes, Atlas says my name again. I blink my eyes open and look—she's definitely not moving.

Two bodies in two days.

How is this my life?

How is death my life now?

I didn't ask for this.

I do not want this.

So why do I have all this chaos in my life?

"It's you… you are bringing death all around me," I manage to say before stepping out of her room and shaking my head.

"Theadora, where are you?"

"You probably killed her too. Didn't you?" I ask him, walking out the same way I came in, being ultra-careful not to touch anything.

"No, Theadora. Now tell me where you are."

"You are the worst possible thing to walk into my life, and I cannot wait until the day you walk out," I say, wiping the tears away from my face, turning and leaving.

I run, run all the way home, and when I get there, the first thing I do is lock my door and hide in my room.

I don't open it even when he knocks an hour later.

Then again when he comes back later that night.

I don't open it at all.

Sometimes you just have to be free from the clutches of someone who doesn't deserve you.

Atlas Hyde. I googled him, and what came up was a lot. There were pages and pages full of information about him. I was surprised, but every picture of him was perfect. Almost too perfect. I wouldn't be surprised if he had a hand in picking what photographs were used as well. He likes to control everything.

Managing to get myself up the next day and ready for work, I open the door with no expectations. I see him standing there, so I shut the door in his face and stand holding the doorknob, unsure of what I should be doing.

"Theadora." I've built up an aversion to the way he keeps saying my name. Always it in fucking full, and honestly, I want to scream at him to stop it. "Theadora, you forgot to lock it." The door is pushed in, and I'm helpless to stop it as he comes face-to-face with me. My hands drop to my sides, my shoulders slump, and I stare at him, wondering why he's here.

"You keep showing up. Why do you keep

showing up?" I ask while shaking my head. "Stop it, Atlas, just stop it. Tell me what you need me to do, and that's it. I didn't agree to any of this. This is not me paying my sister's debt back," I say, waving my hand between us. "I didn't agree to your games. Is this what you do for all your girls, or am I just special?" I ask the question with more venom.

"You have a function at your work next weekend, I plan to be your date." My mouth opens and then closes at his words. That makes no sense. How on earth would he know about that?

He's ignoring all my questions.

Atlas is good at that.

"No. No, you can't be my date. I don't take dates." I step back so there is distance between us. I don't want to be next to him, smelling him, or being anywhere near him. Yesterday, watching him run was bad enough, in his gray tracksuit pants that outline more than they should.

Lord, help me.

It almost made me forget what an awful man he truly is.

Almost.

Then yesterday made me realize how much I despise him.

"Correction… you didn't. And now you do." He turns and walks back to his car. "Who was it…

that you found?" he asks, which makes me believe he doesn't know who it is.

"Mandy," I reply.

He turns around, his hand on the door. "I didn't expect that. I'll clean it up." He gets in and leaves.

I hate him. Really, really, hate him.

Clean it up. What the fuck does that even mean?

But then again, my fingerprints would be on the door and all over my sister's room, so I guess cleaning it up is a good thing. Right?

Driving to work is quick, and when I arrive, Chloe's already there. She is never there this early, and I'm always the first person here so I know. I'm not sure I can deal with her today. I don't know if I can deal with much today, to be honest. My weekend, well, it was one for the books, that's for fucking sure.

You know that book you burn and hope to never see again.

Yeah, that book.

Walking in, I see her at my desk, the computer's turned on, and she's working.

"Chloe." She looks up at me, stunned, shuts the laptop quickly, and stands.

"You come in this early?" she asks.

I look at my desk and see numbers written everywhere. "What are you doing?"

Chloe looks where I am and grabs the papers. "Working out figures. Making sure everything matches."

"Of course it does. Why wouldn't it?" I ask her, confused. "I send them to you every month."

"Because the turnover was down this month," she says, quickly while putting all the paperwork into her bag, then coming to stand near me. "We have the influencer gala next week. I expect figures to be up again by then." She walks past me and doesn't say goodbye as she leaves.

Walking over to my desk, I open the computer and see she has transferred large amounts of money out of the accounts to somewhere else. She's left enough in there to pay salaries but no extra to buy stock, which we will need.

"Hey, why did I cross paths with the evil boss?" Marissa walks in holding two coffees, and she hands me one. Sitting down, she kicks her feet up on the seat opposite me and sips from her coffee.

"Accounts," I say with an eye roll.

"Of course. It's the only time she comes in when it involves money." It is, and they all know it. "At least she didn't ask you to fire any other staff members." She shivers. "That was awful."

"Yep," I say, agreeing. But I don't think that's the last of it. I have this feeling she will be asking me to fire someone else, or maybe even a pile of someones.

"Hey, my brother was asking about you." She smirks, putting the coffee back to her lips. "I know you're seeing someone, but when that ends..." She winks.

"What do you mean, when it ends?"

She looks around the room. "No man can keep up with being this amazing," she says, looking at the flowers. "He's bound to come up short somewhere."

"Oh, he comes up short, do not worry about that." I smile at her.

Just as she leaves, my cell rings. When I see no caller ID, I think it's Lucy, so I answer.

"Mandy has been handled," is all Atlas says.

I don't like it that I know that voice now without even seeing his name. At first, I think he's hung up on me, but when I pull the phone away, I see he's still there on the line.

"She may have family. What did you do?"

"Do you think so fucking low of me," he asks in a voice I'm familiar with. It's his angry tone. "Answer me, Theadora?"

"Why do you care what I think?"

"You're right, I don't. I'll see you next week." Then the line goes dead.

Two days later, another expensive dress shows up for my work event the following week.

I send it back, and don't hear from him again that week.

Peace.

CHAPTER SIXTEEN

Theadora

The police ring me the following week and ask me to go to Lucy's apartment. When I arrive, they tell me that Mandy overdosed, and they ask about my sister. Mandy reported her missing last week, and they want to know if I've heard from her. Just as I am about to speak, the door opens and in strides Atlas himself. He walks straight over to me, grips my waist, and kisses my cheek, pulling me to him. The police officer watches us with narrowed eyes. Just as I am about to pull away, Atlas grips me harder so I'm unable to.

"You two together?" the officer asks, writing something on his notepad.

"Yes," Atlas answers for me.

"I assumed you didn't date, Mr. Hyde." The officer looks up from his pad and eyes Atlas.

"You know what they say about people who assume," he replies.

My cheeks are on fire from where his lips touched me. I lift my hand to see if I can wipe away his touch, but he seems to know what I'm planning and pulls me to him even harder, so our bodies are touching everywhere.

"So, Miss Fitzgerald, your sister?"

"Lucy. We just saw her." Atlas talks for me again, for which the officer eyes him, and then turns back to me.

"Is this true?"

Atlas grips me to him.

"Yes. Yes, it's true."

"Okay, well, either you have to take her stuff or the landlord will get rid of everything."

"Thank you, I will deal with it." I nod, and the officer leaves, leaving me standing in my sister's apartment with Atlas. The last time I was here, I found Mandy dead. And now I am glued to a man who's pretending to be my boyfriend, and who will not let go of my waist, even after the officers have left.

"You can let go now," I say, trying to pull away.

"Did you want to tell him?" he asks, keeping me tight to him.

I'm afraid to look up at him. My hands stay planted on his chest, making sure he can't move me any closer than what I already am. But also, ready to push him away the minute I can.

"I wouldn't have."

"What did she say to you?" he asks.

"Who?"

Atlas squeezes me and lifts my face, so it is now resting on his chest. I can see the flower on his collarbone. He won't let me go, and now my hands are on his pecs.

"You like to play dumb when I know for a fact you are anything but," he states, shaking his head. "Is this a game you're playing with me? Some sort of payback?"

I push off of his chest, but don't get far. He holds me securely against him, and I look up into his eyes.

"If you want to ask me what Lucy said, then ask."

"What did Lucy say?"

"I never said I would tell you." I tilt my head and smile a fake smile.

He bites his bottom lip in frustration and pulls me impossibly close to him. "Are you trying to make me want to dispose of you like I should have?"

"Do it." I dare him.

He looks down at me with his eyebrows pinched together, almost forming a perfectly straight line. "You would rather that than deal with me?"

"Possibly."

"Am I that bad to you?" he asks with sincerity in his voice.

"This is not what I want. This is not what I signed up for."

Atlas loosens his hold, just a fraction, not enough where he lets go of me completely, just enough where I can breathe a little easier.

"You are a good girl, are you not?"

"What kind of question is that?"

"Have you ever done anything bad in your life?"

"No," I answer. "And I don't plan to. And I am more than happy with that choice," I tell him. "Will you let me go now?" I ask, pushing at him once more.

He nods, steps back, and lets me put distance between us. "Lucy has done many things that are bad. Illegal. Can I tell you a bit about her you may not know?"

"I know my sister," I tell him. I may not agree with her, but I know her.

Atlas walks over to the counter and taps his fingers along the top, then grips it as he turns to look at me. "Lucy's been doing illegal shit for quite some time. And it all started with her first hit, when she got away with doing something she shouldn't have. She never learned her lesson, so she went again, and again. She kept chasing a high that's impossible to cure. But she didn't care, and still doesn't. No matter what her consequences are. It's how she's built and how she will continue to build her future. To her, the high is more important than the downfall." He says it as if he knows this better than anyone, as if he knows Lucy better than I do.

"How do you know?"

"My father was the same. Smart businessman, but always chased the high. Anytime he could. And in the end it's what got him, as it will Lucy. She's lucky she is still breathing."

"Is your father still alive?" I ask.

He eyes me as if he isn't sure if he should tell me. "Yes."

"Do you talk to him?" This is the most I have gotten from him in weeks, and as he's giving me the information willingly, I will keep asking until he makes me stop.

His head drops to the side while he assesses me. "Why do you ask?"

"Why can't I ask?"

"My father is incarcerated, where one day Lucy will be too. Because she *will* continue, and one day she will rip off the wrong person."

"I'm sorry about your father, but it seems you're on the way to visiting him permanently too." I smile and head into my sister's room. Finding the closest bag, I start emptying her drawers, throwing her things in there as quickly as I can.

"You have a smart mouth, Theadora."

"So you say." I keep going, walking around, collecting as much as I can carry, because the rest I don't care about. I've already cleaned up enough of her messes. This time is the last. "If it bothers you, you know where the door is."

Hands close around my waist, pulling me back. He's always touching me. Why is he always touching me?

Pulling away, I shake my head, holding my hand up. "Why do you keep touching me?" I ask. "Stop. Just stop with the touching."

"You like it when I touch you. You plan to stand here and tell me otherwise?"

"What…" I reply, confused.

"Every time my hand touches you, you suck in a breath, and your breathing becomes heavy. When I hold you long enough, you calm down and breathe normally, but your heart rate never slows."

"Because you are a psycho," I yell.

He chuckles. "I like touching you. It's interesting." He turns, walking out, and yells back over his shoulder, "Tomorrow at five?"

"Five?" I yell back, not sure what he's talking about.

"A.M." He confirms my running time.

I have started running again every day, and I feel good for it. It makes me feel awesome, and I start my day a little brighter.

How he knows what time I go, I don't even want to know.

I expected him there all week, but thankfully he hasn't bothered.

I really hope tomorrow is the same.

It's not. He's here when I walk out, stretching as I go. I don't talk, my AirPods are in, and I don't want to listen to him at all. I start, and he follows. He takes the same track I do and not once asks any questions. I don't stop this time at the end, I just continue how I normally would. Atlas keeps up, and I can hear his breathing is heavier with each footstep he takes on the way back. When we reach my house, I catch a glimpse and see the sweat beading around his forehead where he has on a cap. His two nose piercings catch the light, and I have to remember to look away.

Opening my door, I don't wait to speak to him. Instead, I go inside and shut the door behind me. He doesn't knock or say a word.

The next day is the same. He runs with me and doesn't say a word. It's becoming nice to have company, even if it is silent. But it's still a little strange as well.

The dress arrives instead of him that weekend. I try to hand it back to the lady with the glasses. She wrinkles her nose at me and shakes her head before she turns and leaves.

My front door opens not long after. "Holy shit! Is that Chanel?" Tina says, walking in as she eyes the bag in my hand.

I smile and turn to her. "Yes, for you." I hand her the bag and watch her reaction. I cannot wear a designer label tonight. No, I have to wear my own label to show it off. It's the whole point.

"For me? Are you shitting me?" she screams,

followed by happy tears. Tina is usually my plus one to this event, and she looks forward to it every year, so I couldn't tell her no. Besides, for all I know, Atlas could pull out, having other plans.

Highly unlikely, my inner voice says to me.

"For you, happy early birthday."

"You can't afford this. So tell me… who got it for you?" She hugs the dress to herself. "And why on earth aren't you keeping it?"

"Atlas bought it, but he's already bought me a few, and I don't want that one. I will be wearing the company's brand tonight."

"You do too much for that company, and they give you fuck all in return," she mutters while shaking her head. "Why you stay on is beyond me."

"It's my career. It's what I'm good at."

"Yeah, yeah, you keep telling yourself that. Plenty of brands would hire you in a heartbeat, Thea, especially with all that experience." She walks off, dress in hand, to my room.

I grabbed the dress from work today that I planned to wear, and when I see it next to the Chanel dress it doesn't compare, not in the slightest, but it will have to do.

"Makeup and hair are on their way," I tell her, checking my cell.

"How is Cruella De Vil? Made you fire anyone

else lately?" Tina asks while opening a bottle of wine, sitting on the edge of my bed, and drinking straight from the bottle.

"No, but..." I bite my lip.

"But what?"

"I feel it's coming. I don't know why, but I just have that feeling."

"Fuck her. Don't do it."

I take the bottle from her hands, taking a long sip. "If it were only that easy."

"It is. You tell her conflict of interest, and if she wants to fire anyone, she can do it."

"She will threaten my job," I tell her.

"Please. You are used to being threatened. Lucy is a chump, making you do what she wants with a little threat. And you always fall down her damn rabbit hole so easily."

"Yep." I agree. If Tina only knew what I was doing, or right now not doing, for Lucy, she would flip her shit. She was the one who pushed me to give up on her last time. Cut ties completely because Lucy doesn't care about anyone but Lucy. And that's a sad fact.

"Atlas said he was coming tonight."

Tina pauses, taking the drink from me. "Do we like him?" She takes a huge drink. "Or... Lucy?" she says with an eyeball, knowing he's in my life because of Lucy but not the reasons why.

"We don't like him."

Tina nods. "Okay, we can deal with that."

Yeah, we can.

If he doesn't kiss me again, that is.

CHAPTER SEVENTEEN

Atlas

Theadora is out the front when I pull up, and her friend, Tina, is with her. I didn't expect that, but I cannot tell her friend to go home, even if I want to.

"Nice dress," I say, stepping out. It's not the one I sent over. No. Her damn friend has that one on.

"Oh, this simple thing," she says, smacking her red lips together. The dress Theadora's wearing is short and red and looks amazing on her body, especially painted on over those hips. She doesn't have unshapely hips like most girls, she has perfectly round and curvaceous ones, with a tiny waist. And that dress? It showcases everything she has to offer.

"Aren't you going to tell me nice dress?" Her friend raises an eyebrow, then waves her hand at me. "I know. You don't have to tell me I look like a million bucks, because I feel it," she says with a cocky smile.

Looking back at Theadora, she's sporting a wide grin at what her friend just said. When she turns to face me it's gone, and it is replaced with the Theadora I have come to know.

"Thea never brings dates. What's so special about you?"

I open the limousine door, then her friend slides in.

"You'll have to ask Theadora that question." I watch as her friend, Tina, looks up to Theadora and winks before she slides over. When I hold the door open for Theadora, she stops and leans in to me. "She doesn't know anything."

"I know," I reply with a smile.

Theadora's eyes flick to my smile, and she shakes her head. "Don't smile, your face may crack." Then she ducks her head to get in, but I stop her before she can.

"Lucy asked about you," I tell her. Theadora's

smile drops, and I wonder if I like that I was the one who made it go away.

Maybe.

"How is she?" Her eyes bore into mine. I look down and cannot see her friend, but I can hear the music that's pumping in the limousine.

"She is Lucy," I reply, explaining as much as need be. She will understand that answer more than anyone. She nods and ducks in without me stopping her this time.

I'm sitting next to Theadora while her friend sits on the side seat. Tina pours herself a glass of champagne, and she turns to face Theadora and me.

"How do you expect to explain him to *them*," Tina asks, raising her eyebrow at us.

"Easy. I'm her boyfriend. Isn't that what you called me?" I tell her, not even bothering to look at Theadora for an explanation, who I know by now is more than likely scowling.

"Oh, yes, Atlas likes to tell everyone that we are together. It's his new thing."

I grin at her words and touch her bare leg which is crossed over the other one. I can feel her tense under my hand, and Tina 'ooohs' loudly.

"We would make the perfect couple, would we not?" I ask Theadora.

Theadora's scowl doesn't leave her face as she looks down at my hand on her leg, and then back again.

"So why are you here again? I know it's to do with Lucy, but no one gets that involved with someone's sister. Let me guess…"

We all go quiet. My hand stays on Theodora's leg, waiting for Tina to speak.

"Lucy owes you money, and you are hoping she shows up at Theodora's?" Tina guesses half right, apart from the fact I already have Lucy. But yes, she owes me money.

"Yep, but I keep telling him he will be waiting a long, long, time," Theadora jumps in with her eyebrows raised.

"Happy to wait," I tell her, giving her leg a squeeze.

Theadora looks at my hand and then back to me. Her eyes are saying something I can't quite comprehend, and maybe I don't want to either.

"So much sexual tension in this car. Maybe I should get out and give you two some alone time." Tina winks.

As we get closer to the event, the car slows, and we get in line with the other waiting vehicles and crawl along.

"Oh, no, do not get out and leave me with Mr. Hyde. He and I are nothing." Theadora turns to me. "Right?" she asks for clarification.

"Right," I reply, moving closer so my breath tickles her neck.

She freezes at my closeness, so I lean down, not able to help myself. I was only going to tease, but now that I can smell her, my lips have a mind of their own and touch her neck, her very bare neck, thanks to the boob-tube dress she's wearing.

She tastes like vanilla, and when I move my lips to taste her just a little bit more, my tongue darts out again and her breathing becomes rapid.

"Okay, I'm out. This is…"

I hear the click of a door, but neither of us moves.

Theadora's frozen to the seat. So I take the opportunity to move around with my lips, and once I get to her chin, I place small kisses everywhere, then move up until I'm near her lips. Those soft, red lips that taste fucking amazing, and all I want is to smash mine on Theadora's and hold her under me as I devour her.

But Theadora despises me, and rightfully so.

I dislike her as much as I want her.

Hands touch me, and at first, they push just a

little before they grip. She opens her mouth, and soon, somehow, she's in my lap. My hands wrap around her waist as she pushes down on me. My cock strains against my jeans as her short dress rides up. I drop my hands a little lower until I feel skin and the top her gorgeous ass. She's got nothing on but a small piece of material, and, if I wanted to right now, I could tear that piece of fabric clean away to make her bare.

Hands push me back as she sits on my lap. The car starts to pull up out the front again—we must have done a lap, and the whole time, all I did was kiss her.

"This, can't happen." She goes to get off of me, but I grip the back of her blonde hair, which is straight tonight, and pull her back down for one last kiss before I feel the car come to a complete stop.

Kissable.

That's all she is.

Theadora shakes me off and pulls her dress down, and I see a glimpse of her black lacy panties before she retrieves her red lip gloss and starts fixing her lips. My thumb wipes the red from my own lips as she looks up at me.

"That has to stop happening. This *cannot* happen." Theadora shakes her head, looking between us.

Moving to the side, she gets out, leaving me sitting there fixing myself up before I can follow her out.

CHAPTER EIGHTEEN

Theadora

Atlas isn't far behind me when I slide out of the limousine. I don't even know where Tina is when I walk through the doors. This year, Chloe didn't want to go all out, so our event isn't as flashy as it usually is. We had to stick to a tight budget, but with what we had, I'm glad it has managed to work out and looks reasonably good.

"Ummm... where is the food?" Tina comes over and grabs my elbow sliding her hand into mine.

"Chloe wanted to save money," I tell her.

Tina rolls her eyes.

Marissa walks over with an edgy look on her face. "Chloe's telling me not to let the food come out until later on. But, Thea…" she looks down at her sparkly watch, "… it's already after dinner and people are hungry." She bites her lip in nervousness.

Usually our events have tables overflowing with flowers and beautiful decorations where you can sit and take photographs. This year, we had to hire an outdoor area with bar stools and smaller tables with only a few flowers scattered around. Marissa and the other girls have been here all morning blowing up balloons to create balloon arches, which we would usually pay someone to do, and they have done a magnificent job.

"Tell them to circulate the food. Where is Chloe?" I ask, putting a hand on her arm to relax her.

Marissa looks over her shoulder and motions behind her. "She's with Jesse."

Of course she is.

Marissa turns and looks at something behind me and her eyes go wide. I turn to see her staring at Atlas, who's dressed like a sex god, standing directly behind me. He steps forward, placing a hand on my hip.

Again.

"Theadora speaks highly about your work." Atlas nods which makes Marissa blush.

"Oh, gosh." She looks at me.

"No wonder you turned my brother down. Look at that," she says louder than she should have. Atlas doesn't let go as she walks away.

Turning into him, I say so only he can hear, "What are you doing?"

"Perfect couple. It's what we are," he says. Then his voice drops. "Make them believe it, Theadora."

Pulling back, I look up at him and see he's staring right at me. His amber eyes are bright as they lock onto mine, and I know he's serious.

Is this another one of his jobs and I'm just a pawn?

"You won't make me lose my job." I shake my head. "I draw the line at that."

He chuckles, but it's dry, then he reaches out, brushing my straight hair back behind my ear as he whispers, "You get no choice in the matter. Maybe in the future, you shouldn't make deals with the devil." Atlas stays where he is, his mouth close to my ear while I manage somehow to catch my breath.

"You are going to ruin me, aren't you?"

"For everyone after me. Yes."

"Atlas Hyde, that can't be you." Atlas pulls back as a woman says his full name.

I try to move, but he grips my arm, pulling me back to him, so I am pinned to his side.

She looks at me, and her eyes go wide. "Lucy's sister, right?"

"Yesss," I say, unsure of how I should answer that.

"She spoke of you. Said you ran a powerhouse clothing company." She smiles.

"I'm sorry, who are you? And how do you know each other?" I ask while looking from Atlas to her.

"Oh, sorry, I worked with her for Atlas." Her eyes flick to him. "Lucy was... interesting."

"Miranda, it's great seeing you, but we must start mingling."

"Yes, of course. Enjoy." She waves us off and walks away.

I turn, looking for Tina and see her at the bar getting as many drinks as she can hold.

"Did you sleep with her?" I ask.

His eyes narrow before he speaks. "Why? Would that bother you?"

I turn and manage to escape his hold as I make my way over to my boss. Chloe is talking to an influencer when I reach her. She smiles and gives me a one-arm hug as she says goodbye to the woman she was talking to.

"You told Marissa to bring the food out?" she hisses.

I feel Atlas push into my back, and Chloe straightens as her eyes land on him.

"I don't think we have had the pleasure..."

Atlas holds out his hand, and she looks at it, then to me for clarification.

"Atlas is my plus one," I tell her.

Chloe's white face tells me she's either shocked or pissed. I'm unsure which emotion is written all over her face right now.

"I know of him," she replies.

"As I know of you," he says back to Chloe, and the way he says it makes my skin crawl.

"Okay, well, I have to go and check on everyone. Is there anything you need?"

Chloe looks to me and shakes her head.

I smile and walk away.

I don't know what's going on there, and I don't want to know either.

I lose Atlas for most of the night, seeing him socializing every now and then. For some reason, he always seems so disinterested in what other people have to say, almost as if he's above them, which he very well could be. Tina sits with him for a good portion of time, but then he disappears. For all I know, he could be fucking that Miranda chick, and I would have no idea whatsoever.

"You ready to go?" Tina asks when I step up to her. She's drunk way too much alcohol, I can tell by the stagger she has going on.

"I have to finish up a few things." I look over my shoulder and Atlas is there.

"I'll walk you out. My driver can take you home," Atlas tells Tina, offering her his arm. She takes it with a smile and looks back at me. "Marry him."

My eyes find his, but he avoids eye contact as he walks her out.

"Why would you bring *him*?" Chloe snaps near my ear.

I didn't even know she was there.

Turning around, her hands are on her hips, and she's mighty angry if her clenched fists are anything to go by.

"You're fired! Fired, Thea." She turns and storms off.

Marissa walks up behind me and says, "Did

she…" Trailing off, she looks at Chloe with her mouth hanging open.

The party is ending, and everyone's leaving so it's time for me to have some fun.

"She did," I confirm, reaching behind me. "Two shots." I point to the tequila, and the bartender is quick to hand them over. I take one, and before I can reach for the other, Marissa drinks it.

"Fuck!" she swears. "Another. Make it a double," she calls out.

Might as well, since I won't be getting paid and now do not care how much of Chloe's money I spend.

Fuck her!

Fuck her right up the ass.

She just fucking fired me.

What the ever-loving fuck!

"Do you plan on drinking everything in the bar?" Atlas asks.

Marissa coughs next to me. "She just got fired, and she does more for that hag than anyone else." I close my eyes at Marissa's words and take a deep breath. The last person I want to know I was fired is him, especially since I'm pretty sure he's the damn reason I got fired in the first place.

He turns to me. "She fired you?"

Looking back to where the shots sit, I take two and down them one after the other, staying right where I am, but don't answer him.

"Yep, she sure did. What a bitch, right?" Marissa coughs. "Okay, well, I may as well quit too," Marissa says.

"No. You will do no such thing. You're the only one who even knows half of what I did at that place."

"Why do you even care? Chloe doesn't seem to care, and you've done so much for that company. No, you fucking run that company."

"Why did she fire you?" Atlas asks.

I turn away from Marissa and look up at him. "Because the company I keep doesn't meet her standards," I reply. My eyes are cold as I feel my heart rate increase, the spite falling from my lips easily.

Marissa's eyes go wide at my words.

"You should go. Thanks again for everything you did tonight." I lean in and kiss Marissa's cheek.

She offers a shy smile to Atlas, who looks back at me before Marissa walks away, leaving us standing there.

"Our ride is here."

"I will find my own ride," I tell him.

He leans forward and stares straight in my eyes. "I will take you home."

Fine! I nod, there is no more fight left in me right now.

He guides me out until we reach the waiting car. When we get in, he doesn't touch me, and I am thankful for small mercies. "I will give you a job," he says. "If that's what you want?"

"No," I reply, not even looking in his direction.

My legs cross over one another as I stare out into nothing. The sky is dark, darker than it should be. It's as if a storm is brewing. When we arrive at my house, I get out before he can help me and don't look back as I make my way up the stairs and step inside. But as I go to shut the door, he's behind me, his hands on my waist, and I have to remember to breathe.

"Atlas." His name leaves my lips as I turn to face him, and when I do, his jacket is no longer on his body, and he's standing there in a white singlet and his dark jeans.

"Theadora..." My name slips between his lips, almost in a whisper.

"We don't like each other," I murmur, stepping closer to him.

Atlas's hand moves up under my breast, and my skin breaks out in goosebumps. He pushes the door behind him shut with his foot and brings his free hand to touch my face. "We don't."

"You should leave," I tell him, but his hands remain on my body. His thumb rubs along my bottom lip.

"I should," he replies.

"But you aren't going to, are you?"

"No. And you really don't want me to either. You need me to help you forget."

"Forget." I say the word as if it's a drug.

Maybe it's him that's the drug, and I could possibly be high right now. Because I don't like him. How can I like a man like him?

"Yes, I'm going to help you forget." Then he does what I never expected him to do, he reaches down and cups my ass, picking me up and walking with me to my bedroom while my legs wrap around his waist. The door is open, so he steps inside and lays me gently on the bed, and my legs ease away from around him. Atlas reaches for my heels and slips them off, then skates his hands up my thighs until he reaches my panties, slipping them down my legs until they're off.

My eyes follow each of his movements, and even though the light in the room is poor, the light from my living room makes it so I can still see him. Atlas pulls his singlet off, and his chest is all I can see. My eyes drink him in, and I wonder how on earth a man like him is in *my* bedroom.

Men with ink have never interested me.

I have quite possibly stereotyped them.

Men who are assholes have never interested me.

I, for sure, have categorized them as bad.

Yet, here I am, in my bedroom, heart pumping hard and wondering when his hands will skim me next. When will his lips make me quiver, now that my breathing is hot and hard?

No man has ever done that to me before.

Not until *him*.

I have never been this nervous in my life, but for some reason, Atlas makes me nervous in every conceivable way possible.

"Stop it!" His hands go to his jeans, and he undoes his zipper as he speaks. "You are thinking way too much." His jeans drop, and now he's naked in front of me.

"No, right now, I am not thinking enough," I say, sitting up and pulling my dress down so I am just as naked as he is. "Maybe after, I will," I tell him, standing, and letting the material cascade all the way to the floor.

"Yes, maybe then we can both think more clearly." He steps forward, his hands touching my naked body.

"Yes, maybe then," I whisper, reaching up so my mouth touches his.

Atlas's hands are gentle, and when we fall backward, his body weight is not fully on mine, but enough so I can feel every inch of him on top of me, even the part I want inside me.

My hips start to move as he grips me. At first, it's soft until he moves them to my neck, then he applies pressure as he lifts and nudges my legs open even farther, one hand on my neck, the other now between my legs. He rubs my clit, and then slides his finger down until he dips inside me, taking my wetness and spreading it over my folds before he does the same again.

"I could play, but right now, I'm an impatient man."

I can't nod nor can I speak.

His hand is still around my neck, and I'm physically unable to move. Atlas grips his cock in his hand and strokes it, then pushes forward so it touches me, not entering me, just touching. I grip at his hands to move, so I can move.

"Tsk-tsk." He shakes his head. "Be a good girl and don't move. We don't want you bruised after the first go, or maybe the second." He winks, making me still, then smiles when he starts touching me again. Moans leave my mouth as his hand leaves my throat and both hands are now on my inner thighs, fingers digging in, probably bruising me.

I go to reach for him. Most positions I have had sex in are usually missionary or doggy. I never wanted more and was happy with both. But Atlas grabs my thighs, turns me to my side, and pulls me down the bed even farther until I feel him between my legs. I go to lift my leg, but he holds it down as he pushes himself closer to me, his cock touching me, and I groan trying to get him to push in just a little farther.

He laughs, and when he does, he moves, and my hand, which was awkwardly at my side, runs through my hair as he pushes in and pulls out.

Holy shit!

One hand moves to touch my clit and rubs while he starts pushing in. My legs close as I try to push back to give him more, open my legs to move more, but he won't allow me to. Atlas holds me still as he pushes, in and out, one hand holding me, the other touching and rubbing me. Just as I am about to come, he pulls out, pushes me flat on my back, and climbs over me. Spreading my legs, he leans down and kisses my breast, bites my nipple hard, then soothes it with his tongue. I moan, loudly, for him. I need more.

Why can't he give me more of him?

Hands grip me again, and this time, in a flash, I am now on top of him. He is on his back as I look down at him. Atlas sits up and pushes my hips down, so I can feel him between my legs, everywhere. I can literally feel him everywhere. In me, on me, and around me.

Atlas Hyde has surrounded me in every possible way and is draining me dry.

Hips move, and hands roam.

When I grip his hair, he doesn't stop me, when I pull chunks of it, he bites my nipple a little harder. Which I fucking love. And when my hips have a mind of their own and start rotating and rocking over him like a teenage girl, he laughs before he devours each breast until I can no longer feel anything but him between my legs. And it feels fucking marvelous.

I feel it coming, that fucking high I have only ever brought on by myself. But, this, well this, is ten times fucking higher, and when he pulls me in, he slams his lips to mine, and I can't stop him. Our kiss is sloppy and messy. I can't keep up with him with all the emotions running through me right now.

"Oh… my… God." I say each word stuttered between his lips.

"No, just Atlas." He smiles against my lips, and I am too high to tell him to shut up or walk away.

Walk, yeah right, that isn't going to happen. Not when my fucking insides are exploding like fireworks.

Bam!

No, it's a fucking eruption!

That's what it's like fucking Atlas Hyde. And even if I regret it straight away, I know one thing for sure, that man has a dick made of solid gold.

Maybe that's why he's rich and so damn ignorant.

"Theadora," he says my name as I come down.

My hands reach out and grip his shoulders before my head lays on it.

I can't move, not even a fraction.

I don't want to move.

My body is spent.

"Get off me, Theadora."

CHAPTER NINETEEN

Theadora

Pulling back, I look at him. His hands leave me and sit at his sides. His eyes are darker than usual as they skim over me. The look makes me feel dirty. I cover my breasts and climb off him. I walk all the way to the bathroom and shut the door behind me, locking it.

Why did I do that?

Why did I have to sleep with a man who could possibly have slept with my sister?

Oh, my God, I don't even need to know the answer to that.

Wrapping a towel around me for modesty, I fling open the door, and he is standing there pulling up his jeans. He looks at me, then away as he reaches for his singlet, pulling it over his head.

"Did you sleep with her?" I ask, cringing at the damn thought.

Atlas ignores me, shoving on his boots.

"Did you sleep with her?" I ask again, my patience growing thin. I grind my teeth as I watch him, waiting for a reply, or even a look so I can assess him. Instead, he collects his things and walks to my door, then looks back.

Goddamn! I hate myself for sleeping with him.

"No. Lucy and I never fucked." Then he leaves.

I stand there, a fraction of a person I once was, and then go after him. The minute I see him getting into his car, I slam the front door shut and lock it.

No more Atlas Hyde in my life.

I'm jobless. I haven't had this problem since I left school. And all weekend I do nothing but dream of amazing sex and wake up wondering what I'm going to do with my life now I no longer have my career.

When Monday rolls around, my alarm clock

wakes me up, but I have nowhere to go. I have enough savings to last me for a few weeks without having a job, but after that, I am fucked. I will be kicked out of my house and have nowhere to go if the bank took it. Literally. My job, the one I loved so much, was my only income, and I have no family to fall back on. The only person I have is Tina, and her house is already full.

I should be searching for a job, but my mind won't allow me to do anything. So, I do just that into the afternoon. Nothing. My cell rings, breaking the monotony, and I answer.

"Thea... I don't know how to do this. Please come back."

"She fired me, Marissa, you know I can't. You can do it. And if you're having any troubles, ring Chloe, I'm sure she can guide you through it," I tell her, which is hard, but this isn't my problem anymore.

"I have repeatedly called her, and when she bothered to answer she was either too busy or didn't care about anything I had to say. How does she not care that her business is failing without you here?"

"Marissa, I would love to help you, but I just can't. I can't give that company any more energy that it doesn't deserve of me. You get it, right?"

She pauses with a sigh. "Yeah, I do." She says no more, simply hangs up.

I feel bad, but I am no longer their pawn to use and abuse.

Jumping on my computer, I finally decide it's time to get my résumé up to scratch and spend the afternoon emailing it out to every job availability I can possibly find, and even to contacts who might have something for me.

When a knock comes on my door, I ignore it. The only person who could be knocking is *him*, and I don't want to talk to *him*. He is the last person I want to communicate with.

"Theadora..."

Okay, that's a girl's voice.

I get up from my couch and open the door. Atlas's girl with the glasses is standing there, her eyes downcast as she reads something on her cell. When she looks up, she looks relieved at first, then angry. "Were you planning to ignore me?"

"Yes," I answer with a fake smile.

"Okay, well, thank you for your honesty, I guess. But I didn't come here to be sassed." She hands me a piece of paper and smiles before she turns to leave.

"What is this?"

"Your instructions are on the card." She walks off, and I tear open the card.

When I open it, I see it is an invitation, and it says it's a requirement.

Fuck!

Dress is fancy, and he asks me to wear heels. A car will be here to pick me up in a few hours.

I've never gotten an invitation before. Closing the front door, I contemplate how I should try and get out of it, but I know better.

I need my sister back.

And once I have her, Atlas Hyde will no longer be in my life.

Atlas doesn't come to collect me. Some man does, and he asks for my cell before I climb in the car. I clutch it, unsure if I should give it to him or not. I sure as shit don't want to.

"No cell phones are allowed, miss. This is not negotiable."

The rebellious part of me wants to scream 'no' at him, and that he can get fucked. Instead, I place my cell in his hand, which he then places in the car, before he comes back and opens my door for me. "If you would, miss."

I do as I am told, and find no one in the car. We drive for what feels like hours before we come to a stop at an airstrip. When the driver opens my door, I see a few other girls dressed similarly to me.

"Please go and wait with the girls." He gestures to them, and I do as he says, walking over to them. They all chatter, and when I reach them, they stop.

One girl, another blonde, walks over to me. "Hey, I'm Ruby." She offers me a shy smile with a wave of her hand.

I have no idea if I should give her my real name or what. So decide to err on the side of caution and only give her my partial name. "Thea," I tell her.

"So, you are new. I have never seen you at one of these before."

"One of what?" I ask.

The plane's door opens, and a few girls start walking the stairs.

"You know… Mr. Hyde's functions. They are legendary, and the tips are worth every dirty thing you do. Trust me." She winks as I follow her up the stairs.

"What is it that you do?" I ask, confused.

She laughs, and she fobs me off. "You're funny… I like you."

I nod, unable to say or do anything else until we enter the plane, and when we do, a few guys are already seated in their seats. It's a private plane, and one of the biggest I have ever seen. Each chair is like a private recliner, and the few men who are sitting on here stare at us with hungry eyes.

"Ruby," I say, leaning in.

She smiles and turns to face me. "Yeah?"

"Where are we going?"

"You don't know?" she asks with her eyebrows pinched together. "Like… really don't know?"

"No. Where are we going?"

"Ladies and gentlemen…" Before she can answer I turn to that voice, it's the girl with glasses. She eyes me longer than the rest when her eyes skim across everyone on board, and then she continues her speech, "Please be seated. You should reach your destination in an hour."

A few girls start walking over to sit near the guys, who, I might add, are all old. As I take the seat closest to the door, my legs start bouncing in agitation, and I bite my lip as I wait. No one talks to me, and Ruby is sitting on the lap of one of the old men as she blushes at something he says.

The only person who seems to have a cell on them is Atlas's girl with the glasses, even then she seems to not care about what everyone else around her is doing.

When the plane finally comes to a stop, she

walks past me, looking down, and gives a slight shake of her head before she walks off. A few people follow her, but I wait until the very last minute—now being the only one left on the plane.

I don't want to get off.

I want to go far, far away, and never come back.

When Lucy is safe, and I have done everything I can to help her, I will be doing just that. If she falls back into the same crowd, I won't be rescuing her again.

They won't be able to find me to do so.

Maybe I will run away to Tahiti and fall between the cracks.

Live some sort of carefree life on a beach somewhere.

When I can't postpone this any longer, I know I have to get up and get off, but something is stopping me.

My legs won't move, and my head is screaming at me to do so, but I can't. I literally cannot move a muscle. I do not know what awaits me on the outside of this plane, and quite frankly, I do not want to know. I want to go back to my house and never leave, remain safe where I was, not out here not knowing what's going to happen next.

I want to go home.

"I see your instincts have finally kicked in." My eyes search for that voice. He stands there dressed in ripped jeans and a white singlet. My head also wonders if it's the same outfit he had on that night at my house. All his tattoos are visible, and I have to look up to his eyes before I get lost in his body.

Amber soulless eyes greet me.

"Your payment is due, Theadora." He turns and walks off, but I hear his boots stop. "If you don't get up and move, I'll chop one of your sister's fingers off." Then he moves, and somehow, so do I. Fast. My feet catch up to him, and when I reach the handles that will help me down the stairs, I manage to look around. White sandy beaches greet me as the sun starts to set, with a crystal blue ocean surrounding us, and I wonder if there is an escape.

When he reaches the bottom, he looks up at me. His eyes search my body—for what, I don't know—before he walks over to his lady, whoever the fuck she is. He bends down and whispers in her ear before he continues to walk. The girl looks at me and walks to the end of the steps, waiting for me to take that final step down. When I do, she offers me her hand.

"My name is Sydney. If you will follow me."

Sydney? Never would have guessed that name.

She starts walking, and I follow. My hands shake at my sides as we walk past a pool that has floating candles and naked ladies surrounding it. "Now, you are to be on your best behavior. This is high stakes, and you will spend the next few days here."

My feet stop at her words. "Staying?" I ask with confusion.

Sydney snaps to a stop and turns to face me. "Yes. You will be staying for the next few days, and there is literally no way you can escape. So, don't piss off anyone." Her heels tap when she starts walking again, and we step up to a grouping of small cabins, each one having a name on it. I see mine as she takes the stairs and stops, turning around once she unlocks the door and passes the keys to me.

"I don't understand why I'm here."

Sydney snaps her fingers. "You aren't special to him anymore. You are here to do what your sister was meant to. So, please stop with the questions, because the answers will not come from me. Your first outfit is already laid on your bed, get dressed and get ready. I will be back to collect you in a few hours." Sydney walks out as I look toward the door.

Breaking down right now is probably not the best option.

But it's the only thing I have left.

Shutting the door, I let the tears that have been wanting to fall, fall unabated.

As I hold myself against the door, I hope and pray this is going to go quickly.

CHAPTER TWENTY

Atlas

"She has arrived." Sydney takes a seat opposite me, but I already knew the minute arrived. "Fair warning, she's crying." Sydney flicks her hair behind her shoulder.

"You like her." I smirk at Sydney, and her eyes narrow in on me. "She's different…" She pauses. "Nothing like her sister, that's for sure," she spits out while shaking her head.

"Yes, Lucy and Theadora are two completely different women," I agree.

"All the guests have arrived. How would you like to proceed with the girls?"

Looking down at my paperwork, I say, "Bring the girls on the east side in first before you bring in the players."

"So, you want me to bring her in last?" She confirms what I don't say.

"Yes. And make sure she doesn't freak out." Sydney nods as she walks out, leaving me sitting in my office getting ready for tonight.

Turning on the cameras, I find the one that's in her cabin and switch it on. I see her sitting at her door with her head in her hands.

I know, you are wondering why on earth would I put cameras in their rooms. Well, this isn't your average holiday resort where rooms are free. No, this is *my* fucking resort, and whatever happens on it, I will know about.

"Sir." Garry walks in, clipboard in hand, as he looks up. "He's requesting all blondes."

Of course, he is. Our highest paying customer usually gets what he wants.

It's the perk of having so much money.

You get what you damn well want.

"Zander always gets what he wants," I tell him, looking back to the screen in front of me. Theadora is now standing, looking at the outfits laid on her bed. She scrunches her nose, and in one swift movement, throws them all to the floor.

"So, I should tell Sydney she's to only send blondes tonight?"

"Yes, only blondes."

He nods as I look away from the screen to him.

My operation always runs smoothly. I've built it that way. It's away from authorities, and it is secluded. The only way to get here is via plane, and I will know the minute one comes within one hundred miles of this place.

My island is just that, mine. And to get an invite here, you either have to be a woman ready to do as I please, or a man ready to spend all his money.

This is an island of pleasure. Nothing else. For both women and men. Some of my biggest gamblers have been women in the past, but I have found it's easier to seduce a man into losing his money than it is to seduce a woman to lose hers.

"Is he ready?"

"Yes, almost. He's drinking with a few girls already. He asked us to replace a redhead with a blonde, and once we did, he was happy."

Customer gets what a customer wants.

They pay millions to spend a few days here, as well as playing in the casino with their own money. Rich people do not care how they spend their money, especially if they have a lot of it.

And Zander has a lot. That's what happens

when you own half the aviation industry, invest in casinos around the world, and still want to dabble. He asked to buy what I have built, but that will never happen. This was my father's idea, and even with the fuckhead criminal he is, it turned out pretty damn good for me.

It's the only good idea he's ever had.

"Get her ready too. I'm sure he will enjoy her company," I say, looking back to the screen.

She's now walking around the room, opening every door, clearly now completely pissed off. And she doesn't even know what is to come.

I hear Garry walk out as she slides back to the floor, her hands pull at her long blonde hair, and she drops her head between her legs. This time it looks like it's in frustration instead of grief.

Remembering the way she tastes, moving is probably not a good idea.

Because if I do, I may just want another.

CHAPTER TWENTY-ONE

Theadora

Sydney knocks on my door, and luckily for her, I am ready. There is literally nothing else to do and nowhere to go. I could explore, but I don't even know if I'm allowed to, and I need to stick to the rules to get off of this damn island.

"You're dressed." I look down at the gold dress that was laid out for me to wear, and when I step out, I see Ruby smiling at me.

"You look so beautiful. Are you excited?"

I look to Sydney who raises her eyebrows as I step down from my little cottage.

"No." I smile, telling her the truth. "Should I be?"

"Yes, you should be." She's wearing a gold dress as well. "You make so much money. Literally, this is all I need to do for work once every six months." My eyes go wide at her words, so I turn back to look at Sydney.

"You excited?" I ask Sydney. She turns her nose up at me and starts walking. It's what I expected from her, but still, she could have at least given me a little more than that.

"Oh, we don't speak to the hostesses," Ruby says, stepping closer to me. "They don't like to make conversation with us. All they do is give orders," she tells me.

"So I have been figuring out," I reply.

Sydney looks back, and I catch a brief smile at her listening to my words.

"You just wait. When you leave with all that cash, you will be smiling."

I doubt it. Because while I am here, I will be paying off a debt I had nothing to do with, and I'm also not out finding a job. Which is a real problem. I need to work. I am not lucky, like most of the people here. I have no one to support me, and no one will care if I died tomorrow.

Fuck.

I am the perfect candidate for shit like this.

Things could go very wrong, and no one would come looking for me, because the only person who cares for me is a friend, and she has no idea where I am.

I'm fucked.

My heels bite at my ankles with each step. The gold dress rubs my skin in all the wrong places, and I want nothing more than to take it off and be in my own clothes. I don't need to check the tag to know it's a designer label.

We enter a foyer that would make a king or queen delighted. Checked marble floors with high ceilings and white walls, white and black tableware with only one splash of color. Blue. People, well, I should say guys, stand around, and all eyes turn to us as we enter the room. Sydney steps to the side as we walk in.

Men of all ages stand in front of us, some with drinks in their hands, others without.

I scan the room, looking for Atlas but don't see him.

Stepping back, so I am next to Sydney, I turn to her. "What am I meant to be doing?" I ask her. She doesn't reply, so I face her. "Sydney! What am I meant to be doing?"

She turns to look at me. "You do whatever it is

the client wants and needs," she snaps. "Now go. You need to make more money than the rest of the girls here." She gives me a little shove in the direction of where all the girls have gone, and I put one foot in front of the other, my heels clicking as I walk.

One guy in particular stares at me, as if I'm the finest whiskey he's ever seen, and I smile. It's all I can manage to do. He isn't old, maybe mid-thirties and good looking. He steps closer to me. "You must be new. I haven't seen you before."

I look past him to Sydney who simply nods her head at me.

"Yes, new," I say, confirming his words. "What is it you're drinking?" I already know the answer, but I reach out for it anyway and take a sip.

He smiles when I hand it back. "Keep it. I'll get another. But you won't get in trouble, will you? Most of the women here do not drink."

Fuck! I forgot about that. Every time I have a drink, Atlas pulls it from my hand.

"It was only a sip, something to take the edge off." I smile up at him.

He nods and turns away, gesturing for me to follow him. I look back to Sydney who gives a little shooing gesture and inclines her head to the guy I am with.

"Is this your first time here?" I ask as we go to a corner of the room.

He waves his hand at a seat, and then he takes the one closest to me. Our knees rub together as he sits.

"No, second. But the first time I only played, as I didn't want to lose concentration. I like to gamble," he admits.

"Don't we all, in some way or another." I smile.

He smiles and seems pleased with my answer as he offers me his drink again. I don't take it this time. Instead, I look around the room and spot Ruby straight away, standing between two guys, her hands are touching the one behind her as she looks up, interested in whatever the one in front of her is saying.

"The girls can get real dirty," my stranger says next to me.

I turn to look at him. He has brown hair with a slight reddish tint. A suit worth God only knows how much, and what seems to be under that suit is a good body.

"You like that?" I ask him.

He pulls his ankle up to his knee and leans back, putting the whiskey to his lips. "As I said, I've never indulged before. Usually, my women are willing."

"And the women here aren't?" I ask.

He looks me over with his bright green eyes. "Something tells me you aren't all that willing, though I could be wrong. You don't indulge like the other women do, nor do you seem to care like they do." He nods to where all the women are located who seem to be throwing themselves at the men. "You do know you could earn a lot of money from talking to someone other than me, right?" he asks.

Fuck money.

"I'm sure I'll survive." I offer him a smile, but he doesn't take his eyes off me as he watches. "What do you do?" I try to change the subject.

"Do you want to get out of here?" he asks.

"Yes."

He stands, offers me his hand, and I place mine in it. The smile on my face is forced as we pass everyone else, including Sydney who gives me a look of approval as we walk out. I look back and see him—Atlas is standing in the corner, observing me.

Turning around, we walk out the door, his hand staying in mine until the cold air hits our skin.

"You're all wearing gold, and strangely all have blonde hair," he points out.

"Should I ask for your name, or is that not allowed?" I ask.

He turns to look at me and smiles. "Nicholas."

"Nice to meet you, Nicholas. I'm, Thea. I would offer you my hand, but you are already holding it."

Nicholas picks up our joined hands as we walk closer to the ocean. "That I am. It's a warm hand, if that counts for anything."

I giggle at his words and realize the smile on my lips isn't false anymore. We stop when the sand gets too much under my heels. Nicholas lets go of my hand and, in one swift movement, picks me up and carries me like a bride farther down the beach.

"You're light." He smiles as I wrap my hands around his neck, so he isn't holding my whole weight.

"It's because I'm starving and haven't eaten. But once I eat a block of chocolate, I'm sure you won't be saying that."

He chuckles, and when we reach the water, Nicholas places me back on my feet.

"Why are you here, Thea? If you don't mind me asking?"

I bite my lip and look out to the waves, the sky is dark, but stars are out, and the ocean looks endless in the darkness.

I shrug. "The money, right?" I smile, placing my hands on the sand as I sit, and he does the same, sitting next to me. "I just lost my job. So this is it till

I find what's next." It's a half-truth, but that's all I can give.

"Losing a job can suck ass. It's what made me start my own company. I have low concentration, and my mouth tends to speak its mind even when I know I shouldn't. So that's why I started my own chain of hotels. My parents were managers of hotels all my life, then I went into them. When they died, I had enough money to buy my first and haven't stopped."

"That's impressive."

Nicholas reaches into his back pocket and pulls out a packet of cigarettes, lighting one up. He offers me one, and I take it. I don't usually smoke, but on the odd occasion when I'm really stressed and can't run I will. Putting it between my lips, he lights it for me and does the same to his.

"So, what type of work did you do?" he asks, taking a drag, then blowing the smoke out in shapes.

"I managed an online clothing boutique. Have done for quite a few years."

"And you got fired?" he asks. "Why?"

"Because the company I chose was only interested in the bottom line. They didn't care about anything. They paid me peanuts for my ability to actually work, and in the end, the bottom line was what mattered." He nods as if he understands. "How long will you be staying at this event?" I ask, hoping to get some more answers than anyone else has given me.

He lays back on the sand, butts his cigarette out, then stares up at the stars. "It goes for a few days. Some leave early once they run out of money. I only stayed one day last time." I lay back next to him, staring up at the stars. "How long are you staying?"

"Till I'm no longer needed," I reply. It's a guess at this point, or when Atlas decides to send me home.

Atlas. I can't even think about him right now.

Because if I do, I'm afraid of what my mind will conjure up.

He played with my emotions, and I let him.

I. Let. Him.

That's the completely fucked-up part of all this.

"You're lost in your head," Nicholas says, making me snap my attention back to him.

"Sorry. I have a lot on my mind, and a lot to work out."

"Yes, the job. Well, if you're interested when this is over, come visit me. I'm always looking for staff."

"I may just hold you to that."

"Nicholas." We both look up as Benji stands

above us with a drink in his hand. "You two look comfortable," he says, offering me a smile.

"You two know each other?" Nicholas asks, sitting up.

Benji brings his drink to his lips and looks at me.

"We do, don't we?" His eyes lock on me before he looks to Nicholas. "I need you to leave, so I can chat with Thea here."

Nicholas stands and looks down at me. "I can walk you back?" he offers.

"It's okay. Thank you anyway."

Nicholas nods before he starts to walk away. I sit up as Benji walks over and takes the spot Nicholas was in. He puts his drink to his lips, then wipes his mouth on his sleeve before leaning on his arm as he looks at me. "You two look nothing alike," he says while eyeing me. "But if I look hard enough, I guess I can see it. Maybe." He looks away, breaking eye contact.

"Who?"

"Lucy." He says her name as easily as I do. As if he knows her more so than anyone else. More than even me.

"You know Lucy?"

He nods. "And you, Theadora Fitzgerald, are her sister, and you're here to work off her debt," he states what I didn't know was public knowledge.

"How do you know, Lucy?" I ask, confused. "And have you seen her? She rang me and told me to stay away from Atlas. But I can't until I know she's safe." I shake my head, "Lucy is always putting herself in situations where she shouldn't be, and I am always there to bail her out. It's tiring being her sister."

"I bet," is all he replies as if he doesn't care.

"Do you play as well?" I ask, changing the conversation. I am going to owe Atlas forever. I suck at making money. Am I meant to be a prostitute and sell myself? I don't even know, because he sucks with his instructions.

"I used, too," Benji says, throwing his glass. I look at it and shake my head. I'll have to pick that up before I go to bed.

"So, why are you here," I ask him.

"Same reason you are, sweetheart." He smiles, looking at me, giving me his full attention.

"And why's that?"

"To get my wife back."

I instantly feel bad for him. "I'm sorry. Does he have your wife?"

Benji nods. "You know her, my wife." He stands and looks down at me. "It's your sister, so don't fuck this up." Then he turns and walks off, leaving me wide-eyed at his words.

CHAPTER TWENTY-TWO

Theadora

I stay on that beach for what feels like hours, the sun starts to rise by the time I finally move.

My sister is married.

That revelation is not something I expected to be hit with.

And how didn't I know?

Isn't that something you tell your sister, your only family you have left?

And why the fuck did Atlas take me if Lucy has a husband to pay her shit back?

My anger reaches a new boiling point.

Who the fuck does she think she is?

I've lost my job. Possibly my home, now that I am not there to look for work, and all because she is a selfish, inconsiderate bitch.

Our parents would be so proud of her.

Not.

Tearing off my heels, I start to make my way back to the cottage, even though I have no idea where the fuck I'm going. This place is beautiful, I will give it that much. The paths are lined with fairy lights and white sand. Palm trees are positioned everywhere, and the gardens are immaculate.

"Lost?" I look for the sound of that voice and watch as he emerges from the darkness like a true fucking viper. He's still wearing that same singlet, and I want to tear it off of him and then scratch my nails down his chest in protest.

"No," I lie, anger dripping from my voice.

"Seems you suck at lying."

"Seems you suck at a lot of things, but let's not go tit-for-tat, shall we?" I raise an eyebrow at him and walk past, hoping I'm going the way I'm meant to.

"Wrong way, Theadora."

I flip him off and keep going. Hearing his chuckle behind me, I keep on walking the path that should eventually take me to my cottage. Hopefully.

I walk for over ten minutes, and my outcome is I'm lost. Very lost.

Sitting down on the ground, I throw the heels somewhere out into the dark. I don't care that they're designer. Fuck them and fuck him.

"What did they ever do to you?" I look back to find Sydney staring at where I threw the shoes. "I mean, they are Italian leather, not cheap." She shakes her head.

"You can have them, I don't fucking care."

"I have them in three different colors." She smiles. I haven't seen her smile before. "Sir asked that I escort you back to your room, and told me that you must be lost." I get up, brushing the sand off my gold dress.

"Do you all call him that?" I ask.

"Yes, he is our boss. What else would we call him?"

"His first name, possibly his last?"

Her eyebrows raise. "No. He prefers it this way. It's showing him respect, and we respect him."

I scoff at her as I walk closer. "I'm tired."

She gives me a look of understanding. "Tomorrow's plans don't start until after lunch, so you have time to sleep." Then she turns, and I start following.

"Am I meant to sleep with these men?" I ask her, cringing as I say it.

"Yes. If you feel comfortable with that."

"Comfortable?" I ask while shaking my head. "I didn't even agree to come here."

"All the women are here out of their own choice. They choose to come and do whatever is necessary to give their chosen man pleasure. And in doing so, that man gives her money and looks after her. You may think we are whoring girls out, but most of these girls come from good backgrounds, and some, well some, are just addicted to sex and chose this as their outlet," she explains.

"I'm neither," I say back to her.

Her eyes zoom in on me through her glasses. "No. I guess you aren't. But the men tip very well, and it will help with your debt."

"It's not even my damn debt."

"You took it on. You agreed to it. So, yes, now it's yours."

"I had no choice."

"There is always a choice, Theadora. Always." She stops and waves to the cottage in front of us, which I now recognize as mine.

"Will you at least tell me how much longer I am here for?"

"Tomorrow may be your last day if you haven't gained the interest of any of the men." She smiles and then walks off.

A knock on my door is all the notification I get telling me it's time to get up. I hear it and look around for the rumple of clothes I threw around last night, finding the one with today's tag on it. It's a short pastel pink skirt with a cream-colored shirt that showcases a lot of cleavage, and a pair of wedges to match. Opening the door, I spot Ruby as she walks past with another girl at her side. When she sees me, she stops as the other girl continues.

"I tried to look for you last night." Ruby smiles, then touches her chin and rubs.

"What happened?" I ask, reaching for her, but she brushes me off.

"It's nothing. Please, don't worry."

"Is someone hurting you?"

"I feel okay. I'm embarrassed by it and would like to not talk about it."

"Okay." I nod, accepting her answer and not pressuring her for more.

"So, where did you go?"

"I went off with a guy named Nicholas."

She grips my arm. "Tell me more. Was he good looking?" I look at her and see pure excitement.

"He was not what I expected."

"They never are." Ruby blushes as we make our

way to the same room as last night, but today it looks completely different. The doors are open, and the flowers are vibrant today, which gives the room a brighter appearance.

Ruby squeezes my arm and walks straight to a guy I saw her with last night. He puts an arm around her and pulls her to his side.

"I see you came back." I turn to that voice and smile.

"I guess I did." Nicholas offers me a bottle of water, unopened, and I take it. "Thanks."

"No problem. The games are about to start soon, feel like escaping again?" he asks, a hint of hope in his voice.

A part of me is screaming at me to say no. Stay. You need to stay here. But then I think this could be the one that pays off your debt. You could be free after this. But then when I look around the room and find Atlas in the middle of a conversation, I know otherwise. He isn't going to let me go until he's had his way. Whatever that may be.

"Yes. We won't get in trouble?"

He chuckles and captures my wrist with tender fingers as we leave. "Trouble is my middle name." He winks, making me smile at his words. "This island has more to do than gambling. Mr. Hyde has made this an island everyone wants to visit. It's whispered about and wanted by many men."

"For the women?" I ask.

"They are a huge bonus, not going to lie."

We walk out, and when we get to the sandy beach, I release his hand and reach down, taking off my wedges, dropping them where we stand, and then putting my hand back in his before we start walking again.

"The women are beautiful, that's for sure," I say as we start walking.

"Not as beautiful as you."

I blush at his words, then I spot some kayaks at the edge of the water and look to Nicholas.

"Do you like the water?" he asks. I nod. I love the water nearly as much as I love running—which I haven't been able to do since I got here.

"I'm not really dressed for water, though." I bite my lip as he pulls his shirt over his head and drops it.

He doesn't have a dad bod, that's for sure; he clearly works out. Nicholas already has on swim trunks, and he reaches for the kayak, pulling it half in the water. "I'm sure you will dry." Nicholas looks to me, and before I can second guess myself, I pull my shirt off and shimmy my skirt down my legs. I'm in a black bra and matching panties, and when

I look up at Nicholas, his eyes are already homed in on me.

I smirk at his reaction.

He coughs and looks away.

"This way, I will be fine." I walk over and step in, and he pushes the kayak out before I feel him get in behind me. He takes us out on the water, and I sit back watching. The ocean waves are calming, and it helps ease my stress just a little bit.

"You seem a bit lost today," he says. "Quiet."

I turn back to look at him, and he's watching me with thoughtfulness in his expression. "I just found out last night my sister is married, and she never bothered to tell me."

"You close to her?"

I shrug. "I'm all she has, and I'm always saving her ass. So you'd think the least she could do would be to send a card telling me."

"I'm an only child, so I would be no assistance in that matter."

"Have you been married before?"

"No. And to be honest, it's never appealed to me."

"Maybe you are searching for the wrong women." I smile.

"You? Do you want marriage?" he asks, throwing my question back at me.

"I thought I did. To be committed to someone and have someone love me unconditionally. But now, I don't know. It's a joke. There are too many people who end up in divorce. So what would be my luck finding my soul mate? To be honest, I have no idea. It seems a pipe dream to me."

"I could see many men choosing to make you their priority. There is something special about you, and it's not just your boobs," he says, making me chuckle. "Though, from what I see, they look great." I smile at his words as we turn around, and when we do, I look back to the shore and my body freezes. "Thea."

"Yeah," I say, biting my lip.

"Do you happen to be in some kind of trouble?" he asks in a hushed tone, even though they can't hear us.

"Ummm… no."

"Well, this will be twice I've been directed away from you."

Atlas stands there on the bank, waiting until we get closer.

"Sir," Nicholas says as he gets out. Nicholas offers me his hand, and when I pull up, I look to Atlas who's staring at me. His eyes skim my body before he looks back at Nicholas. "Leave us," he says.

Nicholas looks at me and rubs his hands through his hair as if he's going to tell him no.

"It's okay, I will hopefully see you later."

"I doubt it," Atlas says.

Nicholas leans in and kisses my cheek before he picks up his shirt and walks away while I stand there awkwardly. Looking for my clothes, I see he has them clutched in his hands, and he's squeezing them. "You take your clothes off for everyone?" he asks with his head inclined.

"Give them back," I say, holding out my hand.

"You like to get undressed for strangers, flirt with them?"

I throw my hands up in the air. "You have to be shitting me, right? Tell me you are joking right now?" I ask in disbelief. "You bring me to this island, for what?" I yell. "For what, Atlas?"

"You are right, you are nothing but a whore." He throws my clothes at me. "Get dressed, you are leaving."

"Why the fuck did you even bring me if you didn't want me to seduce a man?" I pull my skirt up my legs and look at him. "Is this not the whole point of this island?" I huff.

A scream is heard and we both turn.

Atlas takes off before I can, and soon my feet

are stomping behind to catch him as we reach the source of the scream.

My hands cover my mouth as I look down at Ruby, her eyes are black, and her legs are bruised. What the fuck! She wasn't like that a few hours ago. I turn to Atlas who's fast to move, and in two seconds, he has one of the guys up off his feet, and his hands go to his throat, then he throws him back as if he weighs nothing.

I try to stop him but know that's a mistake, as his hands start punching, and soon the guy who hurt Ruby looks worse than her.

A lot worse.

Possibly not even breathing worse.

CHAPTER TWENTY-THREE

Atlas

Wiping the sweat from my brow, I turn back to Theadora and see her eyes are blown wide in horror, her mouth unable to shut as she drops down to the ground where Ruby is lying.

"Ruby. Ruby, please, wake up." Theadora shakes her, but she doesn't move. Pulling out my cell, I call Sydney and inform her of the situation. When I hang up, I look down at Theadora who has tears running down her cheeks as she looks at Ruby.

"Is this what you promote? Is this what you wish would happen t-to m-me?" she chokes on the last words, her shirt now discarded in the sand, leaving her in just her black bra and skirt. I go to step forward, but she holds up her hands. "Go and get help. Don't you dare touch me, you prick."

I step back as our first aid nurse heads down.

Theadora doesn't leave Ruby's side as they assess her. A short time later, Ruby starts to open her eyes, and as she does, tears stream down her face. "It's okay, Ruby, it's going to be okay," Theadora coos to her.

I look to the nurse who nods his head, then signals to the customer who's unconscious next to me.

"Leave him."

Theadora looks up at me with pure animosity in her eyes. If only she knew, she would detest me even more.

"You are going to be okay. But I would suggest someone stay with her overnight to make sure."

"I will," Theadora volunteers.

"You are leaving," I tell her.

Theadora turns to me, her blue eyes angry and holding malice.

"Last night, Theadora," I say.

She nods, standing, leaving her shirt discarded as she grips Ruby's hand while she's laid on a stretcher to be carried to her room.

"It's not that bad," Ruby says, trying to soothe Theadora.

"Bullshit! But I'm still coming."

Ruby doesn't smile, just closes her dark eyes as they carry her out of here.

"You are leaving tomorrow. No questions."

"Why did you even bring me here, hotshot? Why the fuck did you bring me?"

Before any words can leave my mouth, a plane flies overhead and lands. We both turn to it, and when I watch her, I know right now Theadora's going to hate me. Possibly more than she already does.

Jesse and Chloe walk off the plane.

Theadora's eyes go wide, and she turns to me.

"What?" she asks, and then looks back to them. "Why are they here?"

Behind them, when they get off, is an armed guard who has a gun trained on them.

"Did you get me fired?" she asks. "You ruined my life on purpose?"

"No. They ruined your life. Your sister did as well. They just gave me the keys, and I decided to take you for a drive," I tell her, turning and walking away.

Theadora catches up and follows me. As I walk closer to Jesse and Chloe, they spot Theadora straight away, and Chloe has the cheek to at least look a little guilty, while Jesse eyes her as if she's his next meal.

"Why are you here?" Theadora asks. They look down, and she screams, "Why are you here?"

I lean in close. "They owe me a lot of money. You were my way in to finding them. Thanks for that," I tell her.

Her head whips back to me. "I… was your way of finding them? What does that even mean?"

I look to Chloe and smile. "Why don't you tell her?"

"We cheated in one of his casinos, counted and replaced cards," Chloe replies.

"Does everyone rob you?" Theadora asks, looking at me in disbelief. "I mean, my sister isn't very bright, and neither are these two. So how do the dumb ones cheat so much money from you?"

I lean in. "Because they are the only ones dumb enough to try it," I tell her. "But that isn't all now, is it, Jesse?"

Jesse looks down in shame.

"Jesse," I say, and look to Theadora. "Jesse also has a drug problem, and thought that when he took a shipment to transport, he could get away with keeping some for himself. So now Jesse is in a lot of trouble, aren't you?"

"What about the company?" Theadora looks back to me.

"I fired everyone yesterday."

Chloe cringes.

Theodora's head drops.

"Drugs and cheating. Did I really expect anything less?"

"Your sister was the one who actually told me about them. I had no idea who you were until she told me."

"I was the pawn, stuck in the middle?" Theadora asks.

"Yes."

"You wanted to use me this whole time?"

"Yes," I tell her the truth.

"Am I free now?" she asks. "My sister too?"

"Your sister still owes me a lot of money. I was not lying about that."

"Go after her husband," she says, turning and walking off. "I'm fucking out. I don't care. Kill me if you must, but I am out." She flips me off and walks away.

"She didn't know?" Chloe asks.

I turn to her scheming face. "No. She didn't. You just lost the best thing that ever happened to your business." I watch as she deflates in front of me, then my guards take both of them and lead them away.

"What do you want me to do with them?" Sydney asks, watching as they go.

"Get the papers drawn for them to sign all their assets over to me." I hand her the form that lists everything I need. "And make sure Jesse understands that he's lucky to be alive. Show him that."

Sydney nods and walks away.

I look to where Theadora went and walk the opposite way.

It's the right thing to do.

Even if black and white are fuzzy right now.

It is the right thing to do.

CHAPTER TWENTY-FOUR

Theadora

I follow Ruby, it's all I can think to do right now. I don't need to go back to my room because I literally brought nothing with me, and I want my phone back.

"It's nothing, really." Ruby brushes a hand away from her face as they try to ice it.

"You'll still be paid, Ruby. They will be paying for this for a very long time."

Her eyes find mine, and I step forward and clutch her hand.

"We are going home," I tell her.

She manages to smile, but it doesn't last long.

"You can stay with me until you are better if you want."

"I have a home."

"I know, but you need someone to look after you."

"Sir will provide everything. He doesn't approve of his girls being hurt," Sydney says.

"Just me?" I snap at her.

Sydney has enough guilt to actually look away from me.

"Yeah, that's what I thought." I look back at Ruby. "You can stay with me. I will look after you. I have no job now, anyway."

Sydney starts mumbling and then turns to look at us. She passes me something, and when I see it's my cell, I almost sigh in relief.

"The plane is ready to escort you home," Sydney states.

Ruby manages to sit up, clutching at her ribs as she does. I help her stand, as does Sydney.

"Will anyone else be on the plane?" I ask Sydney, who looks up to me as we help Ruby to a wheelchair and start pushing her out.

"No, just you two."

"Good." When we walk out, I spot Chloe, her eyes are filled with tears as she kneels with her hands on the ground. I look away, not caring nor wanting to know what else they have gotten themselves into. Their drama and my sister's drama have fucked with my life, and I have done nothing but try to help the both of them.

As we get to the plane, I turn to help Ruby up and see Atlas standing off on the beach staring at us. My eyes narrow and I contemplate flipping him off, but instead I look away and climb the plane's stairs, having had enough of everything.

I need to get the fuck off this island.

After two days, Ruby asks to go home. I take her, and we say our goodbyes after exchanging phone numbers. I don't hear from Atlas or even his sidekick for the first week. I search for jobs and have absolutely no luck. When I check my bank account to see how much I have left to get some food, I drop my phone to the floor.

The balance reads there is over twenty thousand dollars deposited in my account.

I have never had that amount of money in my life. I work, and I pay my bills, then I repeat.

Atlas's plane was my second ever plane ride, and the first was only due to Chloe not showing up to a meeting, which I had to attend in her place.

Otherwise, we would have lost one of our most influential clients.

Calling Atlas's number, he answers on the first ring.

"You put money in my account?" I practically yell at him through the phone.

"Theadora. Good afternoon. No. I did no such thing. Why would I when you owe me a debt?"

"So, if it wasn't you…" I hang up, not finishing, and search the transaction. In the receipt area, it reads one name—Nicholas.

I start searching for him. He is easy to find, even without a last name. Bringing up his Instagram profile, I see that he has tagged himself in one of his hotels in my city, so I make a call.

"Hello, yes, would Nicholas Brandon be able to speak with me?"

"He doesn't take public calls. Sorry." She goes to hang up on me, so I state, "It's urgent. Please, just tell him my name, and if he doesn't want to talk to me, you've done your job. But as I said, it's urgent. And you don't want an angry boss, right?"

"What's your name."

"Thea. Tell him Thea is calling."

"Hold on."

I wait, walking back and forth to see if he will take my call. It takes a total of four minutes before someone speaks on the other end, "I'm transferring you now."

"Thea." Nicholas's voice comes through the phone. "I see you tracked me down." He chuckles, and it sounds as if he's moving.

"Why did you do it? That's a lot of money," is all I can manage to say.

"We pay each girl who keeps us company on the island. It's how you make money. You left before I could pay you."

"That money should have gone to Atlas."

"I paid him, too, and even asked for your details, but that was a firm no." He chuckles. "That man can be intimidating, but I have been around intimidating men all my life, and I have my ways."

"He certainly is," I tell him.

"So, can I get your number?"

"Do you not have caller ID?" I reply back to him, smiling. "And I can't accept that money."

"Too late, it's yours. And thank you for spending your time with me. Your company was needed." He goes quiet. "Thea?"

"Yes."

"Are you and Atlas a thing?"

"I don't know how to answer that." Which is the truth, as I have no idea.

"Okay, well, I guess I was expecting that."

Hearing a knock on my door, I turn to face it and say, "Can you call me back? Maybe we can meet for coffee or something?"

The knock on my door this time is louder, so I walk over, and I pull it open to see Atlas standing there.

"Yes. I have some free time tomorrow. I will call you then. And Thea? If you don't want the money, donate it," he declares, and then hangs up.

My phone drops to my side as I look at him, his amber eyes are dark and angry while they assess me.

"I checked. You have a lot of money in your account. Did you decide to side hustle on the island?" Atlas's voice is full of malice when he speaks.

How does everyone manage to gain access to my personal life, isn't there laws to stop this shit?

Stepping back, I go to shut the door, but he stops me, holding it open with his foot.

"What did you do for that money, Theadora?"

"Nothing. I did nothing. What the fuck are you doing here?"

He cracks his neck from side to side. "What am I doing here? Maybe we should be asking why you are still breathing?"

"Fuck you." I throw my cell at him, and it hits

him in the chest. He doesn't even blink at my outrage.

"I would like to fuck that temper out of you. What do you say?" He steps forward and makes a move to touch me.

"Been there, done that. What a mistake that was. Never going back there," I say, backing away from his touch. Because he will burn me, and not in a good way. No, his touch will scorch my soul, and I'm afraid of what might happen after that.

"You enjoyed it. We could enjoy it again."

"Oh, sorry, I didn't quite get that memo that you enjoyed it..." I give him an eye roll, "... especially with how fast you ran out afterward."

"It's what I do," he admits. "I fuck and leave. It's what I do," he reiterates it, like I need to hear it or something.

I cross my arms over my chest. "Well, it's not what I do. And it's considered impolite to… 'fuck and leave' as you so disrespectfully put it." I raise my head. "You fuck with people's emotions when you do something like that."

"I'll stay… if that's what you want. But I am not great company."

"I don't even want you here in the first place," I tell him while shaking my head. "So why are we still talking about this."

Atlas reaches out, and I am too slow to stop him from touching me this time. He grips my waist and pulls me to him.

"Stop! Just stop touching me. All you do is touch me."

"I like to touch you."

"You hated me a week ago and were willing to give me to your damn clients," I say as his hands lightly stroke down my arm while he holds onto me.

"I would never have let one touch you. Ever," he whispers in my ear. "Not something so precious." He bites my ear. "So delicious."

I push the door shut behind him, and in the next second my hands are all over him.

I blame lack of sleep—that has to be the reason my mind is allowing this to happen.

Because common sense has gone straight out the window, and in its place stands me, a stupid girl who makes crazy decisions regarding good looking bad men.

Atlas Hyde being at the top of my list.

Actually, he's the only man on that list.

His kisses come in hot and fast while his hands circle and touch everywhere they shouldn't. But like being caught in the ocean, I can't seem to catch a breath unless it's with him, and he is swallowing me whole.

"Theadora."

"Hmmm…" is all I can manage to get out as he grips my ass cheeks and pushes me back so my ass hits the top of my couch.

"You can't hate me when I leave," he says, trailing kisses between my breasts. "I *will* leave, and you can't hate me then."

"I already hate you," I tell him, my hands touching his hair. "It makes it easier." My lips touch his, and I feel his smile on them.

Why am I such a sucker for him?

What is so special about Atlas Hyde that I can't seem to say no?

Yes, he is good looking.

Yes, he makes my body sing every time he touches me.

Yes, when his lips touch me, I feel like I'm on fire, and the only way to put me out is with him. Only him.

"I'm sure it does. Now how the fuck do I get these jeans off?" He pulls at them, and I step back. Getting rid of them, his gaze tracks my movements, and when I look back up at him, I see the bulge that I felt against me.

"We shouldn't do this," I say, shaking my head and backing away. My jeans are off, in a pile on the floor, but my hands and my body aren't touching him now.

The spell is broken.

"Theadora."

"Oh, we for sure shouldn't do this," I say, shaking my head and looking away.

"Theadora, look at me."

I do. My eyes find him, and when they do, I almost weep at the sight.

"Come here, Theadora."

My feet start moving toward him like I have no control, and when I reach him, he wastes no time pulling me back to him, and my body feels him. Everywhere. Because he's completely naked.

"I don't like you."

"I'll stay. I'll stay after," he says, reassuring me.

Lips so soft take mine. There's no hardness in his touch as he places me on the couch and removes my shirt. Atlas's lips move from mine. His body weight presses down on me. I can feel him between my legs, but he doesn't move. Instead, he shifts one of his hands between my legs and starts to rub while his lips touch my breast, his tongue circles my nipple, and I have to remember I don't like this man who's pushing all the right buttons. When he moves lower with his mouth so he is between my legs, I have to remember that it's just sex. And that his mouth isn't sent from the gods, and that he can't be the only person who can pleasure me in this way. Even if I have never experienced anything like this before with anyone but him.

Does he feel the same about me? Am I different? Or, am I like all the others he's been with?

Lost in my own head, his mouth touches me between my legs, my hips buck at his warmth. He chuckles but holds my hips in place, and pretty soon, I have completely forgotten about why I hate Atlas, and instead want him to keep moving.

He does so without any encouragement from me, and I enjoy every second of it.

His mouth does this thing to my clit that has my hips bucking, and he has to grip me harder to keep me in place. No man has ever done this to me, and I have never felt this way before.

Everything about Atlas has my heart pounding in my chest, and my body reacting to his touch. Then I start second-guessing and doubting my behavior, when I know my reactions don't match my constant feelings of loathing for this man.

My hands grip the couch, and soon my body is shaking as an orgasm like I have never had rips through me. With my eyes squeezed shut and my lips glued together, I don't want my scream to break through.

"You can scream. I like it when you scream."

I'm too busy riding my own wave to pay Atlas any sort of attention.

My hips are pulled forward, and my eyes spring open as he hovers above me, his cock in hand as he positions himself at my entrance.

When he looks at me with those stormy amber eyes, I think right then I've fallen in love. But then I realize it's just fantastic sex and snap myself right out of that shit.

Before I can second guess myself, I pull him down, and he smirks before he kisses my chin and slowly works his way down to my neck while he slides into me. My breathing halts for a few seconds when he bites my nipple. Once he's fully seated, I start to move with him, my legs wrapping around his waist and my nails digging hard into his back.

Atlas Hyde fucks me like he does with everything in his life.

With determination, strength, and a passion that is only reserved for things he loves.

Pity I am not one of them.

CHAPTER TWENTY-FIVE

Theadora

Atlas is asleep, and I am wide awake as he lies next to me on my couch with his arms wrapped around me and our bodies close to one another. We didn't speak after the fantastic sex, because what is there to say? 'Thanks for the sex and the mixed feelings you give me, you can leave now.'

Gosh, what have I done?

He moves slightly next to me, and I try to move out of his grip, but he holds me even tighter. Gripping me to him even more as he sleeps.

Atlas is a man who shows next to no emotion.

But when you do get a glimpse of those very few other emotions—not the usual anger—you get lost in soaking it all in.

"Atlas," I say his name, hoping he will wake. I do not plan to lie here, not when all I can think about is what he just did to me and how much I damn well enjoyed it.

His arm that's wrapped around me has a tattoo of a girl licking a gun. I lift it, but he won't let me move it.

"I said... I was staying," he says. "So... I'm staying."

"I need to move, Atlas. I have to use the bathroom."

He grumbles something in my hair and lifts his arm reluctantly. Pulling away from him, I stand and head to the bathroom to clean myself up and brush my teeth, then change into an oversized T-shirt before I walk back out. When I do, I find him in the same spot, his eyes are closed, and a soft snoring sound leaves his mouth. I sit on my other couch and tuck my feet under my ass and stare.

"Theadora," he mumbles. One eye opens, and he jerks his head back for me to come over to him.

"That isn't a great idea," I reply. "Maybe I like it better when you get all moody and leave."

"I don't do moody," he declares, turning on his side and rubbing his face. "Fuck, I'm tired."

"I need a run," I tell him. He sits up and looks at me. "Go run, I'll get something for dinner."

"What if I want you to leave," I ask, then bite my lip.

Atlas stands, completely naked in front of me, then stretches his hands above his head.

Fuck! That body.

"You don't want me to leave," he says, turning and not even bothering to cover himself. His ass is in full view, and I do not care in the least that I am staring. That's one great ass.

"Run. Go."

I don't take orders from any men, but this one is holding my sister hostage, and that gives me no other choice.

But I really do want to run.

Atlas is at my table, and he's managed to put his jeans back on when I return. I pull my AirPods out and look at my table. There's food, and lots of it. Guess he wasn't lying when he said he would arrange for dinner.

"You ordered?" I ask.

Atlas nods and sips whatever drink he has and looks back at his cell phone.

"Shouldn't you be leaving now? I'm sure one of your illegal jobs requires your assistance."

"I actually came here to give you yours back," he says, placing his cell on the table.

"Mine?" I ask, confused.

"Yes. And you can rehire all the staff who were let go. You will get a pay rise above what you should have been paid," he says.

"Did you negotiate this for me?"

Atlas looks back at the food and picks up a burger as he answers, "No. The business is mine now. You were way underpaid, did you know that?"

"Yes. Yes, I knew." I take a deep breath before I decide to move the conversation in another direction.

"Atlas?" I ask. He's mid-bite, so he bites down and starts chewing when he looks up at me while wiping the side of his mouth. "What about my sister?"

"What about her?"

"You still have her. Do you not?"

Atlas puts his burger down and wipes his hand on his jeans. "Come and eat, then we can talk."

"You will talk?" I ask.

He gestures to the food on the table. "Eat, and

yes, I will talk."

I do as he says and pull out the seat next to him.

"You ran for a good hour. Something on your mind?" he asks, picking up his burger again.

"Yes. A lot, actually."

"Such as?" He bites, and I watch in fascination as he eats. He chews silently, and I love that. A lot of men have no idea how to eat silently.

"When is my debt going to be over? What else do you expect me to do?"

Atlas pushes a bag toward me, and I open it to find a burrito, smiling when I pull it out.

"Do you really want it to be over? Isn't your life so much fuller now?"

"Fuller? No. Dangerous? Maybe. Annoying? Yes." I bite into the burrito.

"You have a sexy mouth, and I fucking love to kiss it." Atlas leans over and does just that. His lips push onto mine. It's a quick kiss before he pulls away, making me forget I was even eating.

"Why did you do that?" I ask. "Why are you even here?"

Atlas's cell rings, and he pushes ignore, then looks back at me. "I told you, I like to kiss you."

"Why—" His phone interrupts me.

He sighs and picks it up. I hear fast talking, then his face does this thing I have come to know. It's like he places on a mask where everything shuts down, and back in its place is the Atlas I first met. When he finishes the call, he stands, walking over to his shirt and pulling it on before he turns to face me. "I have to go."

I don't say anything.

"Theadora," he says my name, snapping me out of my trance.

"Maybe it's best you don't come back."

"I plan to come back and sleep in the same bed as you," he says while walking to the door. "Unlock it when I call."

Then he walks out, leaving me sitting where he left me and having no idea what's even happening.

It's almost midnight when I get a message telling me to unlock the door. I contemplate not doing it, or not even replying to him, but I know how relentless he can be. When Atlas wants something, my bet is he always gets it, even if that includes me.

I wait until he knocks, and when he does, my feet are sluggish as I go to the door to open it. Pulling it open, I see his eyes are bloodshot, and his lip is busted. He's changed and is now dressed in a white button-up shirt and dark jeans.

"What happened?" I ask while stepping up to touch his lip. Atlas doesn't back away or even tell me to move, he lets me touch his sore lip as if he's relishing my touch. His eyes even close for a brief second before they fling open and he reaches for my hand, pulling it away from his face but not letting go as he steps inside.

"It's nothing." His voice is soft, so I don't push it. I like it when he's nice, when he's good to me. "I'm tired. I told you I would stay, so I am staying."

"What if I don't want you to?"

"You do," he declares categorically while pulling me along as he heads in the direction of my bedroom. I let him, being too tired to argue with him. When we reach my bedroom, he starts to undress before pulling my covers back. His shirt is already off, and his hands start yanking at the top of his jeans as he looks up at me. "You want to talk?" he asks.

"I want answers."

Atlas rubs his face with his hand, showing his extreme tiredness, but I have put off my questions for long enough.

I want answers.

I deserve answers.

And I am not climbing into that bed with him until I get them.

He finishes dropping his jeans and sits on the edge of my bed, naked. Amber eyes look up at me. "Ask."

"My sister." The two words leave my mouth in a rush.

"I'll let her go tomorrow," he answers just as fast.

Relief lifts off my chest at his words.

"But if she does it again, you won't ever see her again."

My head snaps up.

"She won't."

"You believe that?" Atlas raises one eyebrow.

"She won't," I protest, shaking my head. "Well, I hope not."

"Lucy isn't healthy. She is sadistic and only cares about what she wants." His words are the truth, and I know it. But the fact that he does know that makes me believe he knows her maybe even better than I do, so I ask, "How well do you know her?"

He reaches for me, pulling me forward to him, his head lies on my stomach, and his hands grip my ass. "Well enough."

My hands shake as they lift and touch his hair. He doesn't move, and I wonder if he's even breathing as I start stroking it.

"You were never with her?" I ask, confirming it

one more time.

Atlas keeps his head on my stomach as he answers, "No, never was. Even when she tried so hard," he said. "You know my type… you."

"There hasn't always been just me, and well, we aren't even a type that will stick together. We are bound to break." I go to pull away, but he holds onto me tightly and pulls me back as he lies on the bed, bringing me with him. When I go to get up, he slides me up, so our faces are inches from each other.

"Bound to break," he mutters. "Once I set my eye on something, I usually get it." He leans up so his lips brush against mine.

"Lucky for you I am not a possession."

Atlas pulls back, and then he does it again, his lips brush mine. "But you are. A treasure more like it."

"You trying to sweet talk me, Atlas Hyde? Do you even know how to?" I chuckle.

"No. I don't. I've never had to work this hard in my life to impress a woman."

"Well, you still have a long way to go, because I'm far from impressed," I say back to him, raising my eyebrows.

He pushes up between my legs; all I have on is an oversized shirt and panties, while he is completely naked below me. And believe me, I can feel every inch of him. It's difficult to not move and touch it, because Atlas has an impressive dick, just like the rest of his body.

"You telling me you weren't impressed earlier?" he asks, pushing again. This time I can feel him growing beneath me.

"I mean, in that department… you do okay."

He raises an eyebrow. "Just okay?" Atlas's hands move from my back and slide down, pulling up my shirt so he can slip his fingers into my underwear. "I mean, your screams didn't indicate it was just okay." As I lay on top of him, he pulls my underwear down, and I let him. When they reach my knees, his hand slips between us and he touches my pussy before he smirks at me. "You are so wet. I'm sure *just okay* was meant to be *fucking amazing*."

Atlas slips in a finger, and when he does, my legs part even farther, giving him just what he wants. I can't part them too much, as my panties are at my knees preventing it, but it gives him exactly what he wants, as he's able to slide his fingers out, lift my hips, and push his cock straight into me.

Our eyes meet and lock on each other. He is the first to break away, looking down as he grins and pushes up, sending his cock farther inside me and making my hips start to move.

"Atlas, this can't be anything more than sex," I inform him, reaching behind me to pull my panties off and sit up. He does nothing but give me a smoldering look as my hands grip his tattooed chest, and my eyes shut as I feel every inch of him in me. My hips start rocking, and soon they are bobbing fast. Extremely fast as he helps me, pushing me back and forth in time with my own hips, so my rhythm never slows.

"If you say so, Theadora," I hear him mumble, but I am way too lost in ecstasy to even reply. My hands lift, running through my hair, gripping on while rocking until I feel that perfect build-up. One of his hands leaves my hips while the other keeps me moving, and he reaches up and pinches my sensitive nipple. I crave it and lean forward. He does the same, and his mouth encloses around my nipple, pulling it with his teeth.

I come. I come so fucking hard that I'm pretty sure I see stars.

"There she is," he affirms, throwing me to the bed, turning me over so I'm on my stomach, and he stands, pulling my hips back. He smacks my ass hard, then does it again. I am too sated to move as he lifts me by my hips and slams back into me.

Fuck me.

Literally.

CHAPTER TWENTY-SIX

Atlas

Theadora's ass was made by the gods, her body was sent from hell to tempt and please wicked men like me. And men like me cannot say no to just once. No, we will continue to take and take until there is nothing more to give.

She moans as my cock slides in and out of her already soaking wet pussy. Those moans do mad things to me, and I almost forget to be gentle with her as my hand comes down on her ass again in a loud smack. I expect she likes it because every time I do it, I hear a small moan escape her lips, and her hips rise, telling me she likes it as much as I like doing it to her.

Now, if I could just get my hands around her neck, that would be the icing on the damn cake for me.

The first time I met her, on her knees with a beanie over her head, I had to test it. I had to put my hands around her sweet neck to see how she would react. And she didn't disappoint me. Luckily for me, she never noticed my cock was hard, because if she did, I'm sure all of this would have gone very differently than it has.

She moans loudly as I grip her hair, pulling her head back as I come hard and long. She comes again, and a scream rips from her lips, making my nuts clench at the sound.

I'm low-key obsessed with her.

And she doesn't even realize it.

Pulling out of her, she doesn't move. Theadora's head drops back to the bed, and her heavy breathing takes over while she catches her breath. Standing, I look down on her. Her ass cheeks are red with marks from my hands as she lays there with her legs spread, showing me everything with not a care in the world.

"I won't carry you," I tell her.

She opens her eyes and smirks at me. "I never

expected you to, but now that you mention it, most men in my romance novels carry their women to the bathroom and wash them after they fuck them. You should totally do that." Her body doesn't even move as she speaks, but her lips turn up in a wide smile.

"I won't carry you," I reiterate, this time with more determination.

"You will because I can't walk. So, Atlas, pick me the fuck up, and carry me to the bathroom like a good man should." She turns over, her tits and pussy on perfect show. My cock bounces, ready for another round, and her eyes drop straight to it. "Carry me." She puts her arms out and grins.

"I'm not a good man, that's your first mistake."

Theadora's hands drop, and the smile that was on her face instantly leaves, and, in its place, an intense fevered stare takes over as her face reddens.

I smirk, and, within seconds, I reach for her and throw her over my shoulder, smacking her ass a few times for good measure.

All anger now gone, she laughs as we head to her small shower, and I place her in the cubicle, turning the water on. When I do, she screams as the cold water hits her full blast. Her eyes grow wide as she tries to shift away and cover herself from the ice-cold blast pouring all over her. When she looks up and sees me smiling, she reaches for me and pulls me under, then slams her body against mine for my warmth.

"You are a real asshole, you know that?" she says into my chest.

I turn the faucet, and the water warms because it is fucking freezing.

"And you should probably leave so I can have good dreams. Because if you stay, you are bound to fuck up my happy thoughts of you right now."

I chuckle at her words. "I'm staying," I tell her.

Theadora pulls back and reaches for the soap, then starts washing herself. She looks at me as I stand under the water, and she begins lathering me up. Her hands move in circles over my belly before they dip lower and touch my dick. She smiles up at me and continues to slowly stroke me.

"You should leave. We probably won't get any sleep otherwise," she states, soap now gone and her hand wrapped around my cock as she pulls. She has the perfect touch, and I lean in to kiss her, but she pulls back. "No. You should go, don't you think?"

I bite my lip but stare her down as she maintains her hold on me. "You don't want me to go," I say with a devilish look. "You want to wake up with my cock in your pussy."

She doesn't argue, so I know it's what she wants.

"I want that too. So unless you want me to fuck you up against this bathroom wall with my hand against your throat, I would stop stroking my cock, right now."

Theadora squeezes one last time, then lets me go and reaches for the soap again before she resumes washing herself. I watch, waiting until she's done and gets out before I do the same.

After washing myself, I step out to find her in her bed with the covers pulled up as she lays there watching me.

"Is my debt gone?" she asks.

"Do you want it to be gone?" I ask, drying my hair with the towel while walking over to her bed. She sleeps on an old wooden bed, but her mattress is fucking heaven.

"Yes. I never wanted it in the first place."

"What about me? Do you want me gone too?" I ask while climbing into the bed. I turn on my side, looking at her so I can read her expressions. Her sky-blue eyes close for the briefest of seconds before they reopen.

"I don't know what I want with you. But, Atlas?"

"Yes."

"I don't like you," she says with a straight face. "I don't like you," she repeats again.

"That's okay, most people don't, and I am happy with that."

"Are you, though?" she asks, scrunching her eyebrows. "Happy, I mean. You are a man who I hardly see smile. Are you happy?"

"In moments of time… yes," I answer her truthfully.

Theadora nods as if that's enough.

"'I don't want to owe you anything. I never did."

"You won't," I reply.

"Thank you."

"For what?"

"For not killing me for her mistakes." Theadora yawns and shuts her eyes. If she only knew that I would kill everyone around me before I would ever kill her.

My cell starts beeping, and Theadora doesn't move, so I ignore it and roll her over. She goes easily, and I come up behind her, tucking her into my front. It's not long before she starts to breathe ever so lightly, and it's the cutest thing I've ever heard.

Maybe today she won't hate me.

But soon, very soon, she just may.

CHAPTER TWENTY-SEVEN

Theadora

Atlas stands at the end of my bed when I wake, with a coffee in his hand as he watches me sleep.

"That's creepy," I tell him, sitting up and reaching for it. I take a drink, and he doesn't say a word. "Hey, you... you alive in there?" I snap my fingers in front of his face.

"I don't do this," he says while shaking his head.

"Do what?"

Atlas looks at me as if I should know the answer as his amber eyes bore into me. "I have to go." It's all he says before he turns and walks out.

I listen for the front door to shut before I get up. Searching for my cell, I find it on my bedroom floor, and it's almost dead. Picking it up, I see I have a message from Nicholas. I smile as I read it.

Coffee today? Cannot wait to see you.

My smile drops as I think of the man who just brought me coffee.

But I told him, didn't I?

That I don't like him, and what we have is nothing.

So why can't I have coffee with someone who I met through him?

I write back, 'yes,' and he tells me to meet him in one hour.

Fuck! Jumping around, I quickly get changed to make my appearance worthy, and not looking like a call girl for Atlas Hyde. Oh gosh, how many women does he have? Probably more than I want to know about.

Fixing my makeup, I go to meet Nicholas at the local coffee shop. When I arrive, he's easy to spot. I see his blond hair and tall frame sitting down in a booth, a paper in hand, as he flicks through the pages. Hardly anyone reads newspapers anymore, but I secretly love them.

"Nicholas."

He looks up as I approach and stands, leaning

over to give me a kiss on either cheek before pulling out my chair for me to sit.

This is the kind of man I should be interested in. Nicholas is attractive in every way possible. But why when I do sit, and Nicholas looks at me, I clench my legs thinking about who was between them last night.

"You look good." He eyes me up and down.

I'm not dressed up like I was every time I saw him on the island. Today, I am wearing a pair of jeans and a pink shirt with my handbag crossed over my chest, my blonde hair down and sunglasses on my face.

"Thanks."

Two coffees are brought to our table, and I smile at him. "You ordered?"

"I did. I hope that's okay."

When Atlas does it, it doesn't feel as if I have to thank him; it's like a natural reaction for Atlas. Where this feels different.

"Yes, it's great. Thank you." I smile, putting the drink to my lips and taking a small sip. "I have to talk about that money—"

Nicholas starts shaking his head, effectively interrupting me. "No can do. It's yours."

"I can't accept your money," I tell him. "It's too much. Really it is."

"We have to tip the girls on that island. For one night it's 50K. Trust me when I say it's not enough for the company you provided me with for just a few hours." My eyes bulge as I stare at him, blinking a few times. "You look shocked. How did you not know this?"

"No. I didn't know at all."

He scrunches his eyebrows together. "How didn't you know? Did you come for free?"

"Not really, I had a debt to pay."

Nicholas watches me like he's trying to work it out, but that tilting of his head in concern is only fleeting. "A debt?"

"Yes, to Atlas."

"You call him by his first name?" I bite my lip but don't answer. "Does he allow that?" He pauses when I don't answer again. "We all call him sir or Mr. Hyde, especially on his island. Mr. Hyde is a powerful man," he claims categorically while looking at me. "I guess you are a prize."

I don't like that he says that about me. Prize? I am a fucking woman, not someone's object to be unwrapped and thrown to one side.

"I would have never gone to that island if I didn't owe a debt," I tell him honestly. "And if I knew where I was going, I more than likely wouldn't have gone anyway." I place my coffee down as he nods at my words.

"Fair enough. I'm guessing you won't be telling me about the debt you owe?"

"Sorry, no." I put the coffee cup to my mouth.

"Keep the money. I'm serious. Honestly, it's a thank you for keeping me company and saving me money." He smiles, it is infectious, and I smile back at him.

"I could never."

"Are you still looking for work?" Nicholas asks, folding the newspaper in front of him.

"No. I got my old job back, it seems."

"Oh." He raises an eyebrow. "How did that happen?"

"Atlas."

"Uh-huh." He nods. "I see."

"I don't. I don't understand him."

"You are a beautiful woman. He sees that in you."

"Atlas sees many beautiful women."

"That he does, but no one like you."

We stay and talk a little longer. Nicholas tells me about his work and why he is in town. As we get up to leave, he asks if he can walk me back to my house. I think nothing of it, as I enjoy his company. I tell him about my running, and he jokes about the fact I could probably outrun him. When I laugh at something he says, he wraps a hand around my waist, pulling me to his side.

"Zander."

My head turns fast at that voice.

"Sorry?" I ask, looking from Nicholas to Atlas who is waiting at his car in front of my house.

"Zander, why are you hanging around *my* things?"

Nicholas drops his hands from my shoulders and smirks at Atlas. "You shouldn't call this beautiful woman… *your things*," Nicholas says before he turns and offers me a smile. "I should go. Thank you for coffee, I enjoy your company immensely, and I hope to do it again soon." He looks to the car. "Atlas," he says with a sly grin, and turns, walking off. I watch Nicholas leave, and when I look back at Atlas, his eyes are wide open, set in a glare, his body tense as he stares at me.

"You couldn't wait. Really?" Atlas shakes his head as he spits the words from his mouth like pure venom.

"Wait for what?" I ask him.

Atlas's eyebrows pull down as he locks his stare firmly on me. "You are just like her… more than you realize. More than *I* realized." He turns for his car.

"Atlas! What the fuck are you talking about?"

"You *are* a whore."

My head snaps back, expelling an audible yet cut off breath while becoming momentarily speechless. Once his words sink in, I say, "You did *not* just call me that." I hold up one hand. "You *so* did not just call me that."

"Do you deny it?"

"Dickhead! One coffee with a man I met because of you, does not make me a damn whore."

"Coffee? That's what you like to call it?"

I won't play his games, so I turn away and head to my door.

"I'll see you on Monday," I tell him while opening it.

"No, you will not."

I turn back to look at him. "I could be rash right now and fire you," he says, slipping on his sunglasses and looking in the direction Nicholas walked. "But I've decided keeping you around will be fun. You will see Sydney on Monday and report to her." He gets in his car and drives off, leaving me wondering why the fuck he's so angry. Surely it can't be because of Nicholas. I met the man because of him.

Atlas was true to his word. He wasn't in the office on Monday or all week for that matter. I managed to hire back all the staff I lost, and I have guaranteed their jobs at Sydney's request. She came in once to check with me, then left, and I haven't seen her all week.

When Friday rolls around, I want answers. Like for one, why hasn't my sister called if Atlas let her go as he promised. She cannot be that heartless, surely? She would know what I have had to do for her. What I have had to go through. The least I should get is a simple thank you.

Walking out to my car after work to meet Tina for dinner, I spot Sydney with a bunch of paperwork in her hands as she comes up to the warehouse.

"Sydney."

She stops, huffs, and looks up at me. "Yes."

"My sister…" I trail off the question right there.

"Yes?" She asks, her eyes drilling into me.

"Where is she?" I am hoping for some kind of damn truth.

"Where does your sister go? I have no idea. Shouldn't you be asking her yourself, not me?"

"Atlas let her go?"

She drops her head to the side. "Did he not tell you that was what he was doing?"

"Yes, but…" I look away, then back to her.

"Ohh, I get it. She hasn't even bothered to find you, has she?"

"No."

"Some sister you have there." Sydney walks off and into the warehouse. She has set up her own office, but she doesn't bother anyone and is hardly there anyway. She's actually good to work with because she keeps her nose out of everything.

I'm already dressed to meet Tina, so I go straight to the restaurant. When I get there, I spot Tina at the bar with a drink in her hand sitting on a stool waiting for me.

"Hey." I smile, taking the seat next to her.

Tina's face lights up, and she pulls me to her for a hug. "It's been so long since I've seen you." I chuckle at her words. "How is Atlas? Treating you right?" She winks. "Tell me… have you slept with him yet?" I blush at her words. "Oh, gosh, you have. So, it's serious?"

Most of the men I have been with have been serious, and even then, I wait to sleep with them. But Atlas, somehow, he's different and has managed to crawl between my defenses.

"No, it's not."

"Are you letting your freak flag fly?" she says with a smirk.

"Freak flag?" I mumble, hiding my laugh.

Tina winks as the bartender happens to walk over at that exact moment.

"Two more gin and tonics," Tina orders for us. "Our table should be ready soon. They are busy tonight." I look over my shoulder and see just that; the place is packed. It's a popular restaurant in our part of town, which is about twenty or so minutes from the city. But we like living out here.

"So, tell me all about Atlas."

"Not much to tell, really." I shrug. "We had sex."

"That's it? You just went 'wham, bam, thank you, ma'am' and off you went?"

"More like off he went."

Tina cringes at my words. "Maybe he has commitment issues. All the pretty ones do."

The bartender coughs at Tina's comment, then hands us our drinks.

"Oh, you're pretty too. I bet you have commitment issues, handsome." He nods, then walks off. "See, the pretty ones are the fucked-up ones. And yours is deadly pretty. You know the type… they will singe you with their prettiness."

"Is that even a saying?"

"Fucked if I know, but I am making it one."

"Okay, then." I smile.

"So, he gave you your job back. Are you going to be bringing that up anytime soon? What happened to the evil bitch and her cohort husband?" I told Tina that Atlas acquired the business and gave me my job back, plus a pay rise. She was as surprised as I was and didn't ask too many questions at the time. I guess now is the time for the questions.

"I don't know, and I'm not really sure I care. They not only fucked me over, but everyone who worked there."

"I told you they were bad. I bet it was a gambling debt because you know, Atlas owns that casino in the city."

"Probably." She is right. But that's not my business to divulge. As long as I have my job, I am happy.

"No man does that for just any woman. So don't worry about the sex if you're shit at it." I hit her arm and shake my head. "He obviously likes your pussy to give you your job, and everyone else's, back."

"Maybe."

"No. No maybes about it." She picks up her drink and takes a sip. "So, any news on Lucy?"

All Tina knows is I haven't seen her in a long while, and Atlas was in my life because of her.

"No, still hasn't reached out or anything."

"You need to stop enabling her. I know you have tried, but when she is in a pickle, you always recuse her."

Because I'm all she has.

Or, so I thought.

"I heard she got married. Met her husband, actually," I tell her, thinking about Benji.

Tina's eyes pop wide as she openly glares at me. "Well, holy fuck."

"Yep."

"What a cunt."

I chuckle at her words.

Our names are called, as they now have a table for us. The food is amazing, and by the time we leave, I'm well on my way to being tipsy and happy. Very happy, actually. Friends have that effect on you if they're good ones.

"Theadora…" my name is called.

Tina's hand clutches my forearm as I look in the direction of where my name just came from.

When I see my sister, I freeze.

CHAPTER TWENTY-EIGHT

Theadora

Lucy stands in front of me, one hand touching her other as she gazes at me. She looks good, not like I was expecting after being held captive. Her hair is dark and shiny, her makeup is flawless, and her clothes are designer.

"Lucy," I say in disbelief.

Just then, Benji steps up next to her, gripping her waist as she leans into him, touching his chest with one hand.

"You have some nerve," I tell her. Lucy has the cheek to look down. "No fucking 'Thank you for saving my ass'? Not even a visit?" My voice is rising the angrier I get. I step up to Lucy and attempt to pull at her arm, trying to walk away so I can talk to her in private. Benji grips her tightly, though, holding her to him, so I swing around and say, "You better let her arm go right now, or I will dick punch you so fucking hard you won't be able to walk for a fucking week."

Benji let's go immediately and looks at his wife. She nods as I pull her away.

"Thea," she says, but my legs won't stop walking until we are far enough away that I can scream and yell at her all I want.

When we get to my car, I turn around to face her. Lucy's wearing a black dress that clings to her as she stands straight with no remorse on her face whatsoever.

"What the fuck is wrong with you?" I yell at her. "Where the fuck have you been?"

She shrugs. Fucking shrugs. "With Benji."

"Your husband?" I ask.

She glances down at the ring on her finger.

"Yeah, nice of you to fucking tell me that, by the way."

Dark eyes glance up at me, completely opposite to my light ones. "Would you have even cared?"

My mouth opens wide, and I ask in a shaky, disbelieving voice, "Are you serious right now?"

"You stopped caring what I do a while ago," she points out.

"What? Because I stopped enabling you, I stopped caring, is that what you're saying?"

"You don't enable me."

"I have always supported you, even when you fuck shit up."

"You didn't have a problem doing that with Atlas. You came to the rescue for him."

I point my finger at her chest and push it into her. "You! I did it for you! You ungrateful bitch."

She rolls her eyes at me. "So, are you telling me you didn't fuck him?" She raises an eyebrow.

I notice Benji walking over toward us and turn to him. "You! You can fuck off."

He looks to Lucy who shrugs and starts to walk away from me. I grab her, but she pushes me away, so I snatch her by her long dark hair, pulling her back to me. Benji walks over and touches my arm. I turn fast and punch him right between the legs. Lucy screams, but I don't let go of her hair.

"A thank you is all I ask for, you ungrateful fucking bitch, a simple thank you. You know those two words you have never given me in your life.

Like ever. Even after I looked after you, bailed you out of everything you did wrong. A simple fucking thank you." I pull her hair, so she's in my face. "I'm the only family you have left."

"I love him, and you took him," she screams. "He was mine," she says, trying to get me to let go, but my hands are locked on her hair.

"Who?" I ask, confused, as I look to Benji while he stands there with his fists clenched and his eyes narrowed in on me. "Benji?" I ask, looking back at Lucy. "I would never," I say, shaking my head.

She pulls at my hand until I let go and steps up close to my face. "Atlas! You took him, and he was mine," she screams.

"You're married," I say. I don't understand what she is talking about right now.

"I wanted him first." Lucy's bottom lip puckers out, and just when I am about to say something, the wind gets knocked out of me, and I get pushed backward until I land on the ground.

Looking up, I see Benji with his chin high, and his breathing heavy. He flexes his fingers, then they form tight fists. "You fucking bitch," he says, stepping up closer while I'm still on the ground. "Who the fuck do you think you are?" Benji kicks me, and this time I know I don't deserve that. No fucking way, even after punching him in the balls.

"Oh no, you didn't," I hear Tina screaming. "I'm calling the cops." She has her phone to her ear.

Benji pauses as Lucy steps up and touches his shoulder, calming him down. Once she thinks he's calm enough, she looks down at me. "You deserved that, Thea. You don't get to have everything with a flutter of your lashes. This man, you can't have." She leans up and kisses his cheek, and I watch as his body visibly relaxes at her touch.

Tina drops down next to me, her hands touching me to make sure I am all right before she looks up at Lucy. "I would fucking hate to be related to you, you selfish cunt," Tina says.

Lucy wrinkles her nose and turns, pulling Benji away with her and they walk off. I'm unable to move as I sit on the ground with my ribs aching as I try to catch my breath.

"You're bleeding," Tina says.

I look down at my hand and see I have cut it on something when I fell. "It's okay."

"No, it's not. Stop forgiving her. Lucy does *not* care about you… At. All. And that is clear as she walked away without seeing if you're okay."

She's right, I know it. Problem is, she's still my sister.

"Okay, we need to get you to the hospital. Can

you walk?" I go to stand but scream out in pain when it hurts. "Don't even try that again, I'm calling for an ambulance."

Tina does as she says and waits with me until the EMTs arrive. Once they have assessed me, Tina rides in the ambulance as well while she nervously bounces her leg.

When we finally arrive at the hospital, the doctor comes in and checks me over from head to toes.

"A guy named Nicholas called. He wanted to know what happened and what hospital you're at." Tina hands me my cell, and I see multiple text messages from him.

I write back.

I'm fine, just an altercation with my sister

I don't know if he replies because I turn my cell off and lay back down, trying to relax. My nerves are shot to pieces right now.

"Tell me you will stop, Thea? Please stop seeking Lucy out," Tina pleads.

We've been in the hospital for hours and the pain medications they gave me have finally kicked in. They ended up stitching my hand as I cut it deeply.

"I will."

She smiles, pleased with my simple answer, as the doctor walks back in.

"Your ribs are bruised and can take anywhere from three to six weeks to heal."

Tina clutches my hand as the doctor finishes telling me, "You need to be careful and not do anything that will cause pain."

"Do you want me to call Atlas?" Tina asks as we leave.

"No," I reply, and I mean it.

We head home. I just want some sleep.

My weekend consists of me sitting on my couch and doing nothing. Tina pops in and out and brings me food when I need it, but she doesn't stay long. She's an event planner and has started her own business, so weekends for her are the busiest times. I thank her and tell her not to worry about me every time she slips in for a few minutes.

Flowers also come, and I'm confused as I read the card from Nicholas.

A rose for each tear.

When Monday rolls around, I call in sick. It still

hurts to move, so I let the girls know as well as Sydney I can't make it in. On Tuesday, I do the same, being stuck on my couch and in a lot of pain. On Tuesday night, there is a knock on my door, and when I finally get up to open it, Atlas is standing there, his eyes locked onto mine.

"You don't care for work anymore?" he asks. Then, when his eyes finally move, and he sees me dressed in my robe, he states, "Are you even sick?"

"Yes," I say while lifting one hand to shut the door, but I can't help the grimace.

He stops me and grabs my arm. "Why do you have stitches?"

Atlas enters my home and shuts the door behind him. I take a step back, and he reaches for my robe, opening it, which isn't hard considering it wasn't tied. When he looks down, his eyes zoom in on my ribs and something happens, something about his eyes, and in that moment, I am utterly terrified of him.

Not hand to my throat scared, as I was when I first met him. No, more like run despite the pain. All I can see and hear is Atlas. My body ignores everything around us as I take a tentative step back, ready to make an escape from him to keep myself alive.

His fists are clenched, his brows scrunched in determination as his lips thin in anger. His nostrils flare, and his once amber eyes seem to turn completely black. When he opens his mouth to speak, his voice has dropped even lower. Now it's dark, darker than I ever thought possible. "Who. Did. This?"

I shake my head and close the robe, snatching it away from his grasp.

"Theadora! Who. Did. This?"

"Don't worry, it was an accident." His brows, which were stitched together, loosen as he looks at me. "This involves Lucy, doesn't it?" Atlas shakes his head and steps farther into my home. He walks past me and heads into my living room to stand in front of my television, and then, all of a sudden, he starts pacing back and forth. "Lucy was getting help where she was. I had doctors for her," he tells me, and I am stunned by his words. "She was seeing a psychiatrist I paid for. Your sister has a fucked-up way of thinking."

"You were helping her," I ask in almost a whisper.

"Yes."

"So, why did you make me do everything?"

"She still owed me money, Theadora. I may be a cold-hearted prick, but I always get what's owed to me." And I believe him. "Now tell me… did this involve Lucy?"

"Why does she think she's in love with you?"

He stops moving and turns to face me. "So, you did see her?"

"Yes, I saw her. Tell me, Atlas."

"She only thinks she is because I have been one of the only men in her life who has turned her down. Your sister doesn't like rejection. Actually, she can't handle it at all."

I already knew this. Lucy was like that growing up, and especially in school. If a guy rejected her, she would find a way to make him want her, and they always did. When I had my first real relationship when I was eighteen, Lucy didn't like that, so to spite me, one day when I got home, I caught them in bed together.

Lucy is used to getting what she wants out of men; I guess Atlas was the one exception to her rule

"You never were with her?" I ask again, pulling my robe tightly around my waist but being careful as I do.

"No, never. I don't lie. Your sister doesn't interest me. Most women don't, beyond a bed companion."

I don't comment on that, keeping my lips sealed tight.

"She is married. Why would she do that if she loves you?" I ask.

"I'll answer that when you tell me the truth about what happened," he asks, waving his hand toward my closed gown. "And don't lie, Theadora, I don't like it. What happened?"

"Why haven't I heard from you all week?"

"You are seeing another man, Theadora."

"No, I'm not, Atlas," I bite back. I move to the couch and start sitting carefully, and as I do, he is by my side helping me sit.

"Zander is much like your sister, be careful of him," he tells me, leaning in closer, his breath tickling my neck. As I look up at him, his lips are in front of mine, and I want to kiss them.

"No one is like Lucy. It's next to impossible to be like her." I sit back slowly.

"Just as there is no one like you," he tells me.

My eyes lift to him. "I think you should leave. I will be back at work the minute I can move properly. I have already asked Sydney to bring my computer over, so I can do some work from home."

Atlas stands, brushing his hands down the side of his jeans. "You don't have to worry about work. It's under control," he says, walking to the door and leaving me on the couch. "I'll be back for dinner. Curry it is," he says, stepping out before I can tell him no. He doesn't let me choose. He never does. He just goes ahead and does it for me, and I'm always surprised he seems to purchase what I like.

Curry is one of my favorite foods.

And Atlas is my least favorite person.

That's a lie.

CHAPTER TWENTY-NINE

Atlas

I find it next to impossible to step out of her house, but I need to leave.

What the fuck happened to Theadora? And why won't she tell me?

It has to do with Lucy, I just know it. It's always about Lucy, so I call her cell, and she answers straight away.

"Atlas," she says in a sing-song voice.

"Where are you, Lucy?"

"I'm out shopping, of course, now you don't have me in lockdown."

"As far as I am concerned, you need to stay

locked up, Lucy," I tell her. "It was your sister who asked for you to be let go."

"Thea?" I can almost see the eye roll attached to that word. "You just don't see her for who she is. No one does but me."

"Where are you?" I ask, ignoring her smart-ass comment about her sister. She tells me where she is, and I go to her. When I arrive, she's standing out the front, her bags in hand, sunglasses on her face, while she waits for me in her short, red skirt. Stepping out, she lights a cigarette and smirks as she blows the smoke toward me.

"Have you missed me, Atlas? It's been days since you last saw me." She puckers her lips and blows me a kiss. "What about a kiss for old times' sake?"

"It's sir to you, Lucy…" I pause. "We've never kissed, Lucy, and that's not going to change anytime soon. When was the last time you saw Theadora?"

Lucy's eyebrows rise at her sister's name. "You call her Theadora, and she calls you Atlas. You correct me when I call you by your first name. Why not her?"

"She gets the privilege," I tell her. "Now, tell me, Lucy, what did you do to your sister?" She stands and offers me her bags. "I'll tell you things if you take me for a drink. I'm thirsty."

"Lucy, do not play me for a fool."

"Drink or no info, Atlas. It's as easy as that."

"Where is your husband, Lucy?"

She shrugs. "Working."

Benji and I were once exceptionally good friends. Until he fell in love with Lucy. That was when he lost all his senses, and all he can see is her. He has tunnel vision now and can't see what kind of person she is. Lucy doesn't love Benji, she loves what he gives her. And it's whatever she wants.

"Shouldn't you be spending time with him?"

She pushes her bags to me again. "Drinks, and I will give you the info on my sister you are seeking."

I take her damn bags, and she slides up next to me, locking her arm in mine as we start walking.

"This will be fun. Instead of me sucking up to your clients, I always hoped it would be you buying me drinks instead." She sighs as we walk into the bar. I hold the door open for her as she steps in front of me, entering first. I watch as Lucy prances like she is God's gift to all men and sits on a couch. She pats the spot next to her, but I take the seat opposite. Sitting next to her is never going to happen.

"Do you even care? Not once have you asked me if she is okay." I lean forward, my elbows on my knees.

"The fact you are here tells me she's fine." Lucy smiles and waves down a waiter, ordering two drinks for herself, and she looks at me. I shake my head as he leaves to get her order. "Tell me, Atlas, what is it about her?"

"She is everything you aren't," I tell her honestly.

Lucy's mouth opens and closes, her eyes narrow as she leans forward. "I'm more. Better than her. Always have been," she tells me.

"You aren't. But typical of you to think you are."

"Fuck you!"

"Oh, so that's your sore spot. Why?" I ask her out of curiosity.

"She gets whatever she wants. Even the things she doesn't want, she gets."

"From what I've seen, Lucy, your sister hardly asks for anything, and works damn hard for what she has." My anger has spiked at her words.

"You are blind to her, most men are. It's why I have fun stealing them away from her." She smirks.

"You're married, Lucy."

"So it seems," she says, looking down to the ring on her hand.

"Tell me, Lucy, do you love him?"

Her eyes gloss over as she smiles. "A little. But not as much as I love you."

"You don't know me enough to love me, Lucy. Now, tell me about what happened to your sister."

She throws her hair over her shoulder as the waiter puts her drinks down. I pay for them, and he leaves, then she picks one up, drinking it and looking at me over the rim of her glass.

"She was mouthing off at me." She shrugs. "Pulled me away from Benji and started screaming."

"Why was she screaming?"

"Why do you want all the details?" she questions.

"Tell me, Lucy."

"Okay, okay. Then Benji came over, and as he pulled her off me, Thea had the nerve to whack him between the legs and knock him to the ground. He couldn't even get it up that night, thanks to her," she whines.

"How did she end up with bruised ribs, Lucy?"

Lucy waves her hand. "Benji was not impressed with what she did, so he knocked her down and kicked her."

My feet are moving before anyone can stop me. I can hear Lucy saying something behind me, but I don't give two fucks. I drive straight to Benji's house, knowing that's where he works from, and when I don't find him there, my fists start slamming into walls and trashing his desk.

He laid hands on her.

He hurt her badly.

He will pay.

Calling him, my hand stops punching shit when he answers, "Atlas."

"You laid hands on Theadora?"

"She deserved it. She had her hands on my wife," he replies.

"Your wife is an evil bitch, and you fucking beat an innocent woman who did nothing but look out for her sinister fucking sister."

"She fucking punched me in the balls. She deserved the beating she got. She's lucky that was all I gave her."

"You better hope I don't see you soon, Benji, because I'm going to do to you what you did to her, plus more."

"Atlas, we are basically brothers."

"I don't give two fucks. You drove over the line in the sand." I hang up, and when I leave, I leave a trail of lighter fluid on the floor, and when I walk out, I let the match drop.

I let myself into Theadora's house when I arrive back. She's curled up on the couch watching a movie. I sit next to her, pulling the table closer so we can eat.

"You don't have to stay if you don't want to. Tina comes and visits, and she brings me food every day."

"She's a good friend," I tell her. As I finish speaking, the door opens and in walks Tina. She smiles when she sees me sitting next to Theadora and takes one of the opposite seats.

"You got food already," Tina asks, tucking her feet underneath her. "Good, saves me ordering."

"Eat, I brought plenty," I say, nodding to the food laid out on the table. Theadora nods encouragingly, and Tina does just that, helping herself.

"I saw your sister today," I say, looking at Theadora. She pauses and looks to Tina, then back to me.

"How was she?"

"Nope. No, you do not care. Her husband beat you up, and she stood there as if you weren't hurting at all. Fuck Lucy, I say."

Yep, she's a good friend, that one. Theadora chose right, Lucy is fucked-up in every way possible.

"She just stood there?" I ask Tina.

Tina nods before replying with, "Yep. That's one hell of a bitch—"

"I survived, that's the main thing," Theadora interrupts before picking up another piece of chicken and placing it in her mouth.

"So, Atlas, tell me your intentions with my girl." Tina smiles mischievously, then wiggles her brows.

I turn to look to Theadora to see she's already watching me. "What intentions do you want?"

"I haven't figured that out yet," Theadora replies.

"Okay, one step at a time."

We eat, we laugh, and when I walk Tina out, she threatens me with bodily harm if I upset or hurt Theadora.

I definitely like Tina, and I don't like many people.

When I walk back to Theadora, I lean down and pick her up. She goes to wrap her arms around my neck, but flinches when she does so.

"I thought you weren't one of those guys who does this?" she teases as I get to her bedroom and lay her on the bed as carefully as possible.

"It seems I make exceptions for you."

"Why do you think that is?"

"I will do nothing but break your heart,

Theadora. They called me 'the heartbreak' for a reason growing up."

"Heartbreak me, and I will heartbreak you, Atlas Hyde. I've had enough of that to last me a lifetime, and the next time someone hurts me, I won't sit by idly and just let them."

"Unless it's your sister, right?" I get undressed and slide into bed next to her.

She groans at my words. "You're starting to sound like Tina," she mumbles.

"Tina is a smart woman."

"I'll tell her you said that. I'm sure it will make her head big, though."

"Tell me where I can touch you," I ask, whispering in her ear.

She pauses and looks at my hovering hand above her, her soft fingers grip hold and pull it down so it touches her stomach, and then she covers it with her own fingers.

"No higher," she says.

"And no lower?" I ask.

"Gentle," she speaks, answering me.

I push myself closer to her, so my front is on her back while my hand skims down her stomach to her panties. Pushing them to the side, my finger touches her folds. A soft moan leaves her lips, and she attempts to move.

"Stay still, or I'll stop," I tell her.

Theadora shakes her head, but she listens.

I push a finger in and kiss behind her neck until I get to her ear, biting it. "I like you, Theadora Fitzgerald." When I kiss around to her jaw, I see her eyes are shut as she answers me, "I like you to, Atlas Hyde." She whispers like it's a truth she never wanted out in the open. "But you are still an ass."

I chuckle at her words and push my finger in hard. She moans as my thumb presses on her clit, circling it slowly. Pressing in and out, I insert another finger, and she moans louder.

I feel her come not long after, when her sweet pussy tightens around my fingers, and she tries hard to stay as still as she can while moans leave her mouth. Pulling my fingers out, I resume where I was next to her.

"Have you thought maybe it's just about the sex," she whispers.

"It can't be," I tell her honestly. "I have sex with different women, and none make me come back like you do."

"That isn't very encouraging, knowing you are fucking other women."

"None since you." I watch her breathing stop at my words.

"I've had enough hurt to last me a lifetime,

Atlas." I don't say a word, because that's not something I can guarantee her. "So, walk away if you think you will break my heart before it's too late," she whispers.

But that's impossible to do.

To walk away from her.

I've tried and failed.

CHAPTER THIRTY

Theadora

Atlas goes to work and comes back every night that week, and every time, he brings me food. Tina stops after the second night, knowing he's doing it, and she smiles as she leaves. They like each other, and I like that they do. Atlas doesn't like many people, but, for some reason, he seems to like Tina.

On the weekend, I start moving more, the pain being much less and almost tolerable now. I tell Atlas I will be going back to work, but he looks at me as if I have grown a second head and instantly starts shaking his.

"That's not going to happen," he says with victory in his tone as if he's won a fight I didn't even know we were having. He places the food in front of us, as he does all the time, and starts eating, then he pushes a glass of water my way. He kicks his legs up on the coffee table and switches on the television.

"This is weird. Is this not weird?" I ask, looking at how comfortable he is. His cell starts ringing, and he studies it before he answers, his eyes on me, ready to answer my question.

"Hello." He continues to watch me. "Yes, soon." He hangs up, not breaking eye contact. "What is weird?" he asks me finally. "Us?"

I nod.

"Is this not what you want?" He indicates with his hand between us.

"You can't ask me that. We don't even know what we are. How do you start something from something so wrong and dark?" I ask him.

"So, you want this to end?"

I scrunch my brows. "I didn't say that."

"But you indicated it."

I shrug. "They say you shouldn't be sleeping with your boss anyway."

"That's an excuse. You know your job is safe, no matter what."

"I don't know that," I argue back.

"For fuck's sake, Theadora…"

"Yes, Atlas?"

He stands, frustrated. "I have to go to work, and I guess I'll go home after."

"Home? You have one of those?" I ask. "How come you never take me there?"

"Is that the problem? That you haven't seen my house?"

I shrug, looking away. It's not *the* problem, but it's also a part of himself that he keeps away from me. While he can delve into all of my affairs, it seems a bit unfair that I know very little about his personal life.

"Get dressed, you're coming with me to see what I do, then you're spending the night at mine."

I look to the food and don't move.

"Theodora, get dressed. Or do you want me to pack your bag for you as well as dress you?"

I stand, and he watches me as I walk into my room.

Tina brought me some nice button-up shirts and black leggings. I put them on carefully and sit on the bed to slide my boots on. When I stand, Atlas walks over to me and starts doing up my buttons at the front.

"My men will be surprised to see you," is all he says, doing up the last button. He leans in and kisses my lips softly, then pulls away, picking up the bag I packed. I follow him out until we reach the front door.

His car is parked out front behind mine, and he holds open the door as I get in, then does the same.

"Why? Why will they be surprised to see me?"

Atlas turns to face me and shakes his head, "Because last time they saw you, they kidnapped you," he says matter-of-factly. My body starts to shake at that thought. "They will never hurt you again."

"Do they do that often, kidnap people?" I ask.

He cracks his neck as he drives. "Only those who need it."

"I didn't need it. They took me from work, and I didn't even know why at the time. I didn't deserve it."

"Unfortunately, you are related to *her*."

"Yes, very unfortunate," I reply. My cell rings and I see Tina's name.

"Hey," I say, as we drive up to his casino.

"Hey, was going to pop in, but wanted to see if you needed anything first."

"Umm…" I look to Atlas as he slows the car down to park. "I'm staying at Atlas's house tonight," I tell her.

"Ohhh… is he putting on his big boy undies

and taking this relationship further?" I turn to Atlas and see him smirking, obviously overhearing what she's said.

"I guess so."

"Okay, good. I expect a full report tomorrow."

"Okay," I say with a smile.

"Thea, remember if you take it up the ass to use heaps of lube," she yells.

I hang up on her and turn to see Atlas in full smirk mode.

"She's trouble that one." He gets out of the car, walks around the front, and opens the door for me.

"The best kind of trouble, though." Stepping out, he nods and starts walking toward the casino. The doormen let us in, and Atlas takes us to a private elevator. When we fly up to the top floor, I see Sydney sitting out the front at what I guess is her desk. Her eyes skim me before they go back to Atlas. "Are you sure she should be here?"

Atlas looks to me and tips his head toward Sydney. "She will keep you company. I won't be long."

Sydney looks up at me, then turns back to her computer. She's never one to talk much anyway.

Two guys come out of the elevator we just did and walk up to Sydney, totally ignoring me as I sit on a couch in front of her office area. The floors are wooden, and Atlas has two large doors that go into what I'm guessing is his office. Sydney has an almost full glass desk with a computer and not much else.

"Sir, in?"

"Yes, but he's busy right now, so take a seat and wait."

Both men turn, and when they do, they spot me. I look up and recognize one straight away. I didn't get a good look at the two guys who took me that night, but their voices I would know anywhere, and these two are definitely them.

One smirks as he walks over, and he sits relatively close to me. "Miss." He nods to me.

I look over at Sydney to see her already monitoring us with watchful eyes.

"I know who you are," I say, smiling, but not making eye contact.

"Is that so, miss?" the other answers.

When I turn to look at them, they are both staring at me.

"Yes, that is so."

"Well, Atlas always has a new flavor of the month. I guess you're lucky to be this month's."

"I guess so," I answer.

"Barry, Leo… office, now." We all turn to Atlas, who we didn't even hear standing at his office door, and he's staring at us. They both stand immediately and nod to me as they pass, heading into his office. Atlas looks at me, then shuts the doors.

I look to Sydney.

"They are painful, both of them. It's why they're so good at doing his dirty work, but they always listen." She turns back to her computer. "So don't worry about them."

I wait for what seems like an hour before the two guys walk out, they both nod in my direction, but don't offer another word. After that, Atlas walks out, and behind him is Benji, who looks worse for wear. Benji's eyes lift to me, and I flinch when I take in his face. His lip is busted, and both eyes are black.

Atlas walks over and stands in front of me as Benji passes, and as he does, I close my eyes, waiting until he is gone.

I thought of him as a nice man the first time I met him.

How blind men can be made by love.

"He isn't an awful man, he's just gotten lost in your sister," Atlas says to me.

I look up once the elevator doors close, and Benji is gone.

"But what he did is unacceptable," Atlas states. He helps me stand and leans over, kissing my forehead before pulling us away and heading to the elevator.

I look back to Sydney to see her watching, a soft smile on her face, one I have never seen before, but I look away when she spots me staring.

Atlas's house is big, but did I expect anything less? When we slide out of his car, the doors open, and a lady is standing there dressed in jeans and a shirt, and she takes the bag from Atlas's hand, holding the doors open for us to enter.

"Madge, my maid," he says as we walk in.

Atlas's house is between my house and the casino, not too far out of town, but enough to be away from the hustle and bustle. The exterior has a large wrap around driveway, which is basically a circle, so you can stop in front of the house, then keep driving out if required.

Walking inside, you are met with high ceilings and coolness. No joke, I literally feel cold standing in his house. His living room is sunken, and on the wall is a large-screen television. Two couches, which are brown and look very uncomfortable with pillows thrown over them, surround it. There's one small coffee table in the middle. His living room is probably the size of my entire house.

He walks me farther down a hallway and into a room with another set of double doors. When I look in, I see a king-sized bed, which is obviously custom made. The mattress is sunken into the wooden frame where you could put a coffee next to you on the bed. It's amazing.

He walks over to a door, opens it, and places my bag in there, and that's when I see his walk-in closet.

"This is where you live?" I ask.

He walks over to me and nods his head to the bed. I sit on the wooden part as he leans down and starts to remove my shoes.

"I have a Jacuzzi I have never used. Want to test it out with me?"

My stitches are healing, and I can use my hand again now. My ribs aren't as sore, so when he says that, I nod my head with encouragement, the warm water will feel awesome on my body.

"I didn't pack a swimsuit," I tell him.

"You don't need it." He starts to undress, and I look at his door, which is open. "She's left already. She leaves the minute I get home unless I need something," he says, referring to his maid. "We have food on the counter, and you and I are going to explore each other very tenderly in the Jacuzzi, aren't we?" he asks, raising one brow.

"Explore?" I say with a smile.

"Oh, yes, explore we will." Atlas steps forward once my leggings are off and helps me remove my top. The bruising is almost gone, and I can now lift my arms above my head without flinching too much, but he always helps, he has done all week.

I'm falling a little more each day for him.

And I'm doing nothing at all to stop it.

Kisses are spread all over my lips once we're both naked. He turns, pulling away, and grips my arm as he walks to where he wants me to go. Stepping through a door, he presses a button and the shutters open, showcasing a Jacuzzi out under the stars. It has fairy lights everywhere and is the most magical thing I have ever seen. On the table next to it are two champagne flutes.

"This is beautiful," I state as we walk outside.

Atlas helps me in, then he steps in and brings me back so I am sitting on his lap in the water. I can feel him between my legs, but he doesn't move, he simply hands me a glass and whispers in my ear, "I could get used to this."

My heart skips a beat at his words. Used to what? Me? Or us doing this? I don't want to ask him what we are, because I still don't know, and I am getting used to this side of him.

CHAPTER THIRTY-ONE

Theadora

Atlas has changed, this much is obvious. He isn't the same man who had his hand around my throat and told me I had to pay back my sister's debt. No, he is a man who feeds me, looks after me, and doesn't give me a choice or wants a thank you. He has become a constant in my life, which I've only ever had one of —my best friend.

Atlas tried to keep me in his house, but when Monday came around, I went back to work much to his dismay. He takes me every day and picks me up every afternoon. Some nights he drops me back home or leaves me at his house, mainly because his business is run at night. But every time he does, he makes sure I have food, and I feel safe before he leaves.

When Friday rolls around, as I walk out of work, I see him standing by his car instead of waiting in it like he usually does, with his ankles crossed and his hands in his pockets as he stares at me.

I smile at him.

"Where can I get myself one of those?" Marissa asks, knocking my shoulder, laughing. She offers a small wave to Atlas, who doesn't return it but offers me a smirk I know all too well.

"Fuck, you look good," he whispers in my ear as he pulls me to him and kisses my earlobe, biting it before pulling back.

"Do you have to work tonight?" I ask, hoping he doesn't. I want him in my bed and doing awful, bad things to my body, which he hasn't been doing. He will only use his fingers and mouth, no cock, because he's afraid he will hurt me. I'm no longer afraid of that. I want the hurt that will come from him. Want it. Need it. Badly.

"Yes, but you can guarantee when I finish, I'll be banging on your door."

"I can drive myself, you know?"

He opens up my door, then smacks my ass. "I know, but this way I get to touch that ass every day before I have to work."

"You can do more than smack it. You can reach between it and fuck me with your cock."

His eyes go wide at my words. "You want to fuck?"

"Yes, I want to fuck." I smirk, getting in.

He softly shuts the door and walks around to his side, getting in and taking off.

My house isn't too far away, and when we arrive, I turn in my seat to look at him. "What are we?"

He shakes his head.

"Think about it. Please. I would like an answer when you get back." I climb out without touching my lips to his. He waits until I reach my door before he drives off.

Opening my door, I'm met with darkness. Switching on the lights and kicking off my shoes, I walk deeper into the house. A noise stops me before I go any farther, and when I look up, the first thing I see is Nicholas sitting on one of my sofas. His leg is kicked up over his knee, and there's a smile on his pretty face as he looks at me. My body freezes as I look at him.

He has nothing in his hands, and the only sign of danger is that he's in my fucking home.

"Nicholas."

His smile grows wider. "Thea. I've been waiting for you."

I clutch my keys in my hand. "Why are you in my home?" I start stepping back when I hear a muffled cry, but I can't see where it's coming from. "Nicholas, who is with you?"

He shakes his head, that smile never leaving his face. "Do you honestly think I would let someone hurt you?" His teeth are showing, and it isn't a pleasant sight.

"What are you talking about?"

Nicholas stands, takes one step forward, and I take one step back. There's a couch between us, so he will have to jump that to reach me. I'm sure I could reach the door in time before he caught up with me.

He holds his hands up in the air. "I would never hurt you, Thea. Never." Nicholas keeps his hands in the air.

"Who is with you?"

He nods to the couch I can't see in front of. "Look for yourself."

So, I do. I lean over, and when I do my eyes go wide at the sight before me.

My sister and Benji are both tied down with gags in their mouths as they sit on the floor in front of the television.

"I couldn't wait for you to start their punishment. So, I cut their hands and broke their ribs to show them what you went through." He looks down at Lucy. "She was very willing to tell me everything that happened to you, even bragged about it," he snarls at her.

My hand flies to my mouth as a strangled cry leaves me. I look to Lucy to see her eyes are full of tears, and she looks at me for help.

Benji keeps on looking at Lucy like he can save her. He can't. Lucy isn't as tied up as he is. Benji has extra rope around him, so his bindings are tight.

"You think they will learn their lesson?" he asks.

I look behind me, hoping someone will help. But no one can. It's us, and that's it.

"Nicholas, you need to let them go."

He waves at them. "They can't walk, and I haven't finished teaching them not to touch what is mine."

"I'm not yours, Nicholas."

His eyes fixate on me, and his smile drops. "You think Atlas loves you? He doesn't." Nicholas looks at his watch, then back to me. "He should be in an accident... right... about... now," he draws out.

"So we can go wherever you want. Lucy told me everything. He was using you and making you do things you didn't want to do. I would never, Thea, ever make you do that. I would treat you like the queen you are."

"What did you do to Atlas?"

Nicholas looks back to his expensive watch. "He was bound to have an accident with the way he drives." He winks as Lucy whimpers. His eyes flick to hers, and she flinches. "She loves him, did you know that? She told me to kill you and not him."

My eyes find hers, and she looks away. There is no guilt whatsoever. I know he's telling the truth.

"I can kill her for you. Make it slow and painful."

Lucy looks to me now, her eyes wide and pleading. A part of me wants to walk out my front door and pretend this never happened. Unfortunately, that part that is always saving her won't let me.

"Don't hurt her, Nicholas. Let them go."

"No can do, Thea. They need to understand." He walks over to them, leans down to Benji who is fighting against his ties, and pulls out a knife. In one quick movement, he puts it to his throat and slices. Benji falls to his side as the blood pools on my floor.

I scream; it rips out of my throat.

Nicholas doesn't even look up as he moves on to

my sister. Before I can move, my front door is kicked open, and Atlas walks in, his mouth is bloody, and his hand almost looks twisted. His eyes find mine before they move to Nicholas. When he goes to do the same to my sister, she manages to move, but Nicholas is fast and stabs the knife straight into her leg, smiling as he stands.

"You've come to play too?" Nicholas bends down, reaches for the knife, pulls it out of Lucy's leg, and wipes it on his black trousers before standing. "If they can't kill you, I guess I'll have to, so we can be free to be together." Nicholas looks to me, and I lean over and spew on the floor right in front of me, which makes my ribs scream in protest.

Atlas walks toward him, reaching for something in his back pocket as he gets closer. He lifts and shoots straight between Nicholas's eyes while I watch as he drops to the floor.

I do the same. When I can manage it, I crawl to where my sister's slouched. Touching her neck for a pulse, I can feel she's still breathing, barely. But she has lost heaps of blood. I look up at Atlas, who walks over to Benji and tries to stop the bleeding, but I know it's too late. He's gone almost white.

"Call an ambulance," I manage to scream at him.

Atlas looks at me, and his eyes are vacant. "This is your fault," he spits.

I press on my sister's leg and reach for the blanket on my couch, wrapping it around to stop the bleeding.

"I hope she dies on you, Theadora," he says, reaching for Benji, picking up his lifeless body and walking out.

I look back, hoping Atlas will come back in, but he doesn't.

He leaves me sitting on my floor with my dying sister, and a heartbreak that I didn't know I could possibly feel so strongly.

Atlas did as he said he would.

He's heartbroken me, so now it's my turn to heartbreak him.

To be continued…

ABOUT THE AUTHOR

USA Today Best Selling Author T.L. Smith loves to write her characters with flaws so beautiful and dark you can't turn away. Her books have been translated into several languages. If you don't catch up with her in her home state of Queensland, Australia you can usually find her travelling the world, either sitting on a beach in Bali or exploring Alcatraz in San Francisco or walking the streets of New York.

ALSO BY T.L SMITH

Black (Black #1) FREE

Red (Black #2)

White (Black #3)

Green (Black #4)

Kandiland

Pure Punishment (Standalone)

Antagonize Me (Standalone)

Degrade (Flawed #1)

Twisted (Flawed #2)

Distrust (Smirnov Bratva #1) FREE

Disbelief (Smirnov Bratva #2)

Defiance (Smirnov Bratva #3)

Dismissed (Smirnov Bratva #4)

Lovesick (Standalone)

Lotus (Standalone)

Savage Collision (A Savage Love Duet book 1)

Savage Reckoning (A Savage Love Duet book 2)

Buried in Lies

Distorted Love (Dark Intentions Duet 1)

Sinister Love (Dark Intentions Duet 2)

[Cavalier (Crimson Elite #1)](#)

Anguished (Crimson Elite #2)

Conceited (Crimson Elite #3)

Insolent (Crimson Elite #4)

Playette

Love Drunk

Hate Sober

Connect with T.L Smith by tlsmithauthor.com

KISSES AND LIES

USA TODAY BESTSELLING AUTHOR
T.L. SMITH

SAMPLE OF KISSES AND LIES

Chapter 1

My hand grips the glass tightly, my breathing picks up as I watch Marcus Stone in action. I can see his skin glistening under the cold night as each stroke grows more powerful, one after the next. My eyes are glued to his body as he comes up for air. His strong jawline opening then closing with each powerful breath.

How can watching someone swim turn you on?

I'm not sure, but it can. Somehow, it turns me on.

Bringing the glass to my lips, I take one more drink, finishing the contents and feeling the burn as it goes down. I need the liquid courage. I need it to face him.

Marcus turns, his strokes finally stop when he looks at me. The light from the kitchen is not helping to obscure me while I sit in the dark, stalking.

My breathing stops as his two powerful eyes lock on mine, his strong hand lifts and strokes his fingers through his hair. I'm helpless, compelled to watch as the muscles in his arm flex during the simple action. His hazel eyes narrow in on me.

"Rochelle…" Marcus says my name as easily as the water drips from his body.

It makes me even madder.

The drink in my hand feels like it could smash any second with the pressure I'm applying to the glass. He pushes himself out of the water, his body glistening as he comes to a stand not too far away from me. Reaching for a towel, he wipes his body. His hazel eyes, now darkening, lock on me when I don't answer him.

"I'm leaving you," I say with a smile when my breath doesn't hitch at those words.

"This is what you want?" Marcus asks.

No fight.

No argument.

Nothing.

"Yes. I'm leaving you," I say it more to myself this time. Perhaps to help me believe it.

He chuckles.

The asshole chuckles.

"Off you go, then."

With as much strength as I can muster, I throw my glass at him, just missing his head when he ducks out of the way. When he stands taller, I know that was a mistake. But I honestly don't care. I can't care anymore.

Pushing myself up from the lounger where I was reclining while working up the courage to tell him I am leaving, I step forward and come just under his chin.

Marcus is tall.

I hate that about him.

I hate a lot about him.

But then again, I also don't.

"Is that all you've got to say?" I arch an eyebrow.

Marcus arches one back. "Yes." Then he pushes past me, not caring that he almost knocks me over as he heads inside.

I follow. I shouldn't, but I can't help myself.

"You sleep with her… when I'm not here… in this house," I yell.

He halts, turns, and smirks. "I do," Marcus says, the towel now dropping. His swimwear is sitting low on his hips. "And I fuck her hard… all the ways you hate and I love." His lips turn up, waiting for me to say something in return.

"I hate you," I spit at him.

"I know you do."

"I hate you sooo much."

"That's okay. You can leave now."

"Is she coming over?" I yell.

Marcus turns, his hand touching the railing that leads up to his room.

I've never really lived here—I was simply a visitor. No one important. Just a person in this man's life. No one can penetrate him. I feel sorry for the person who finally does get through his impervious walls. They will either be very stupid or love him more than anyone else ever has.

"She will be now. I have steam I need to work off." He takes the steps two at a time and disappears, leaving me standing in the foyer with my hands clenched as I look around for my things. Luckily for me, I never moved out of my house. What a mistake that would have been if I had.

But worse, what a mistake Marcus was.

While rushing around and grabbing my things, I hear a ding. Looking over to the countertop, I see his cell light up. For some reason he doesn't have it locked, so I slide it open and up pops a girl's name.

> **Misha**
>
> Today 9:30 PM
>
> I want you to spank me so bad, baby.

I gag, then throw his phone

at the floor, hard enough that it shatters.

Fuck him and his cheating ass.

Picking up my bags, I walk to the door and step through, pushing it hard behind me so it slams. Again, fuck him and whatever he thinks.

My car is parked out the front where I left it when I arrived to break this nightmare off. I knew I'd have to make a quick getaway.

I need to get away from him.

He's poison.

Toxic.

A virus that has inserted itself in my system and won't leave, sucking me dry.

Now is my chance to extract that poison.

I have to for my own health.

For my own good.

Marcus Stone is not good for me, that much is obvious.

Throwing my bags in the car, I look back at his house, and when I look up, I see him standing on his balcony staring down at me. Marcus' hands are on the railing, his eyes locked onto mine.

"Fuck you," I say under my breath as I walk around and get into my little red car.

The car creaks, and I wonder if it can hear my own heart doing the same.

KISSES AND LIES IS AVAILABLE EVERYWHERE NOW!

Printed in Great Britain
by Amazon